The Silen

The Silent Oath

Copyright © 2025 **Desh Yadav**

All rights reserved. No part of this book may be reproduced, distributed, or transmitted in any form or by any means, including photocopying, recording, or other electronic or mechanical methods, without the prior written permission of the author, except in the case of brief quotations embodied in critical reviews and certain other noncommercial uses permitted by copyright law.

This is a work of fiction. Names, characters, places, and incidents either are the product of the author's imagination or are used fictitiously. Any resemblance to actual persons, living or dead, or actual events is purely coincidental.

First Edition

Published by **Desh Yadav**

For permissions, requests, or inquiries, contact: **deshnjoy@gmail.com**

Table of Contents

Preface 1
1: The Breaking Point 4
2: The Flight That Changes Everything 8
3: Shadows of the Past 12
4: A Storm Brews 16
5: The Confrontation 19
6: The Long Drive 22
7: The Grip of the Past 28
8: A Silent Warning 32
9: No More Battles to Fight 35
10: A Step Too Far 39
11: The Door That Shouldn't Open 43
12: The Choice She Didn't Make 47
13: The Shadows That Follow 51
14: The War She Never Saw 54
15: The Man Who Didn't Fear Him 58
16: The Ghosts He Won't Name 62
17: The Game She Wasn't Supposed to Play 65
18: The Moment He Stops Waiting 68
19: The Moment He Strikes 71
20: A Love That Needed No Words 75
21: A Love That Needed No Permission 79
22: A Love That Lived in the Smallest Moments 82
23: A Love That Needed No Proof 86
24: A Love That Didn't Need to Be Said 90
25: A Love That Felt Like Forever 93
26: A Love That Wrapped Around Her 96
27: A Love That Couldn't Be Undone 99
28: A Love That Stood Still 102
29: A World That Demanded Perfection 105
30: A Throne She Never Asked For 110

31: A Test She Didn't Know She Was Taking 116
32: A Throne That Came With a Price 120
33: A Storm Waiting to Break 124
34: The Truth He Could No Longer Hide 127
35: The First Move Was His 130
36: The Moment the Game Changed 133
37: A War That Just Became Personal 136
38: The Night Everything Changed 138
39: The End That Wasn't the End 141

Preface

Some promises are made in silence, binding the soul more than spoken words ever could.

The Silent Oath is more than just a story—it is an exploration of power, love, and the dangerous secrets that shape lives. When I first envisioned this book, I was drawn to the idea that silence often holds more weight than words. That what remains unsaid can be more powerful, more dangerous, and more life-altering than any spoken truth.

This book is for those who have ever felt trapped in a world that wasn't meant for them. For the ones who fight their way out, for the ones who find strength in the shadows. Elena's journey is one of resilience, of discovering her own power, and of learning that silence can be both a prison and a weapon.

As you turn these pages, I invite you into a world of intrigue, danger, and passion. A world where trust is fragile, love is tested, and power is never given—it is taken.

Thank you for stepping into *The Silent Oath*. May this story stay with you long after the final page.

Desh Yadav
2025

The Silent Oath
1: The Breaking Point
2: The Flight That Changes Everything
3: Shadows of the Past
4: A Storm Brews
5: The Confrontation
6: The Long Drive
7: The Grip of the Past
8: A Silent Warning
9: No More Battles to Fight
10: A Step Too Far
11: The Door That Shouldn't Open
12: The Choice She Didn't Make
13: The Shadows That Follow
14: The War She Never Saw
15: The Man Who Didn't Fear Him
16: The Ghosts He Won't Name
17: The Game She Wasn't Supposed to Play
18: The Moment He Stops Waiting
19: The Moment He Strikes
20: A Love That Needed No Words
21: A Love That Needed No Permission
22: A Love That Lived in the Smallest Moments
23: A Love That Needed No Proof
24: A Love That Didn't Need to Be Said

25: A Love That Felt Like Forever
26: A Love That Wrapped Around Her
27: A Love That Couldn't Be Undone
28: A Love That Stood Still
29: A World That Demanded Perfection
30: A Throne She Never Asked For
31: A Test She Didn't Know She Was Taking
32: A Throne That Came With a Price
33: A Storm Waiting to Break
34: The Truth He Could No Longer Hide
35: The First Move Was His
36: The Moment the Game Changed
37: A War That Just Became Personal
38: The Night Everything Changed

1: The Breaking Point

The scent of stale whiskey clung to the air, mixing with the faint aroma of burnt toast. Elena Rossi stood in the doorway of the kitchen, gripping the edge of the counter as she watched Luca Moretti fumble with the coffee pot. His back was to her, his shoulders tense, the worn fabric of his shirt stretched too tightly across his frame.

"Elena!" he barked without turning around. "Where's the sugar? Or do I have to do everything myself?"

Her breath caught. She'd forgotten to refill the sugar jar after yesterday's grocery run. It was a small mistake, but small mistakes never stayed small with Luca.

"I—I'll get it," she said quietly, stepping into the room.

"Of course you will," he muttered, slamming the empty jar onto the counter. The sound made her flinch, though she tried to hide it.

She grabbed the unopened bag of sugar from the pantry and handed it to him, her fingers trembling. He snatched it without looking at her, his movements jerky, impatient.

The man before her was a ghost of the Luca she had married. Once charming and full of life, he had become someone she barely recognized—someone she feared.

"Elena," he said suddenly, his voice cutting through the silence like a blade. She froze mid-step, her heart pounding.

"Do you even do anything around here?" he continued, turning to face her now. His bloodshot eyes were sharp, cold. "I work all day to keep this place running, and you can't even keep the basics stocked?"

Her mouth opened, but no words came out. She wanted to defend herself, to remind him that she worked too, balancing a part-time job with managing their tiny, cluttered apartment. But she knew better than to argue.

Luca took a step closer, his towering frame casting a shadow over her.

"You're lucky to have me, you know that?" he said, his voice low, menacing. "No one else would put up with you."

The words hit harder than she expected, even though she'd heard them before. She clenched her jaw, refusing to let the tears prickling at the corners of her eyes fall.

LATER THAT NIGHT, AFTER Luca had passed out on the couch, his snores filling the room, Elena sat in their cramped bedroom with a suitcase at her feet.

The bruises on her arm, hidden beneath her sweater, throbbed faintly. They weren't the worst he'd ever left, but they were enough. Enough to remind her that she couldn't stay—not anymore.

Her best friend Sophia's voice echoed in her mind: "Elena, you don't have to live like this. You deserve better. You deserve to be free."

Elena looked at the framed photo on the nightstand. It was from their honeymoon, taken on a sunny day by the Amalfi Coast. In the photo, Luca was smiling, his arm around her shoulders, his face full of love and hope.

She no longer recognized that man.

Taking a deep breath, she zipped up the suitcase and slipped out of the bedroom. Her hand lingered on the doorknob for a moment, a wave of fear washing over her. What if he woke up? What if he stopped her?

But then she thought of the nights she'd spent crying herself to sleep. The mornings she woke up dreading the sound of his voice.

Enough, she told herself.

She opened the door as quietly as she could and stepped into the cool night air.

THE TRAIN STATION SCENE

The platform was nearly empty, save for a few late-night travelers huddled on benches. Elena pulled her suitcase behind her, her steps slow, hesitant. The station lights cast long shadows on the cracked tiles, and the hum of the arriving train filled the air.

She hesitated as the train doors opened. This was it. If she got on that train, there would be no turning back.

Her phone buzzed in her pocket. She pulled it out, her heart sinking as she saw Luca's name on the screen. For a moment, she stared at it, her thumb hovering over the "decline" button.

Then, with a deep breath, she silenced the phone, tucked it back into her pocket, and boarded the train.

As the train pulled away from the station, Elena stared out the window, the lights of Milan fading into the distance.

For the first time in years, she felt a flicker of hope.

2: The Flight That Changes Everything

The Flight Scene

The turbulence came without warning.

Elena fumbled with her book as the plane jolted, her cup of water tipping dangerously close to the edge of the tray table. Before she could catch it, the cup fell, splashing its contents onto the dark gray trousers of the man seated beside her.

Her heart sank.

"I—I'm so sorry," she stammered, reaching for napkins.

The man looked at her, his sharp gray eyes betraying no emotion. His tailored suit and calm demeanor made him seem untouchable, like someone who didn't belong in economy class.

"It's fine," he said, his voice smooth but distant.

Elena flushed, unsure if his response was genuine or dismissive. She quickly cleaned up the spill, avoiding his gaze. But as the flight continued, she couldn't shake the feeling of his attention lingering on her.

When they landed, Dominic glanced at her luggage tag as she reached for her bag. "Elena Rossi," he murmured under his breath, the name now etched into his memory.

The Hotel Scene: A Sudden Encounter

The hotel lobby buzzed with travelers dragging suitcases and exchanging conversations in half a dozen languages. Elena stood at the reception counter, her pulse quickening as she gripped her phone. The receptionist, her perfectly tied bun and polite demeanor unwavering, had just delivered news that made Elena's stomach twist.

"I'm sorry, madam," the woman said, her French accent clipped, "but your reservation was canceled three days ago."

"That's not possible," Elena replied, her voice trembling. She turned her phone screen toward the receptionist, showing the confirmation email. "Here's my booking. I didn't cancel anything."

The woman frowned, but her tone remained professional. "I understand, madam, but the reservation no longer exists in our system. And unfortunately, with the fashion expo, we are completely full."

Elena's fingers curled around the strap of her handbag. She stepped back from the counter, fighting the lump rising in her throat. Every hotel app on her phone showed the same result: No availability.

Her chest felt tight, her thoughts a whirlwind. What do I do now?

The weight of everything—the canceled booking, the long flight, the months of struggle—pushed against her like a tidal wave. Her vision blurred, and she blinked rapidly to hold back tears.

Then she felt it.

A presence.

"Elena Rossi," came a low, steady voice from behind her.

She froze, the sound cutting through her spiral of emotions like a blade. She turned, and there he was—the man from the flight. He stood tall and composed, his sharp gray eyes meeting hers.

"All good, Miss Rossi?" he asked, his tone smooth and unreadable.

Elena opened her mouth, unsure how to respond. He was just as imposing as she remembered, his tailored suit immaculate, his hands casually in his pockets as if he owned the room.

"Y-Yes," she stammered finally, though her voice betrayed her.

Dominic nodded once, his expression impossible to read, and stepped past her toward the elevators. His presence lingered long after he disappeared from view.

Before she could process what had just happened, the receptionist reappeared.

"Madam, I must apologize," she said, her tone suddenly warmer. "It seems there was an error in our system. While the hotel is fully booked, we've arranged a nearby luxury apartment for you. It will be fully covered as compensation."

Elena blinked, startled by the abrupt shift. "A luxury apartment?"

"Yes, madam. Here is the keycard," the woman said, sliding it across the counter with a practiced smile. "Your driver is waiting outside."

Still stunned, Elena accepted the keycard and headed for the car waiting by the curb.

THE APARTMENT SCENE: A Smoke in the Night

The car ride was short, but Elena barely noticed the city lights blurring past the window. Her mind replayed the moment in the lobby—the man from the flight, Dominic Moreau, appearing at the exact moment she'd felt like breaking.

How did he know my name?

Her thoughts were interrupted as the driver pulled up to an elegant apartment building. The façade gleamed under the glow of the streetlamps, the architecture modern but understated.

"Here we are, madam," the driver said, stepping out to open the door for her.

Elena stepped onto the pavement, her heels clicking softly against the stone. The apartment building loomed before her, pristine and intimidating. She hesitated for a moment, adjusting the strap of her handbag and pulling her small suitcase behind her.

As she approached the entrance, the low purr of an engine caught her attention.

A sleek black Rolls-Royce Phantom pulled up to the curb, its polished exterior gleaming under the soft Parisian light. For a moment, Elena simply stared, her suitcase forgotten in her hand.

The tinted window of the Rolls-Royce rolled down smoothly.

Inside, Dominic sat with the same unshakable composure she'd seen on the flight and in the lobby. A cigarette rested between his fingers, the faint glow at its tip casting a warm light against his sharp features.

He took a slow drag, his movements deliberate, and exhaled a spiral of smoke that curled into the cool night air.

Their eyes met.

Elena's breath caught, her grip tightening on the suitcase handle. She wanted to look away, but his gaze held hers, sharp and unwavering.

"Miss Rossi," he said, his voice carrying easily over the distance.

Her heart raced, though she couldn't explain why. She didn't answer—she wasn't even sure she could.

Dominic tilted his head slightly, as if he were studying her, then gave the smallest of nods.

"Good night," he said, his tone smooth but dismissive, as though the encounter had been entirely hers to process.

Before she could respond, the window rolled back up, and the Rolls-Royce pulled away with a soft growl of the engine, disappearing down the quiet street.

Elena stood frozen for a moment, the night air cool against her flushed cheeks.

Who was this man?

Shaking herself out of her daze, she turned and entered the apartment building. As the elevator doors closed, her mind was filled with questions she couldn't yet answer.

3: Shadows of the Past

The rain had started in the early hours of the morning, a steady drizzle that blurred the Paris skyline through the apartment's floor-to-ceiling windows. Elena sat at the small dining table, her laptop open in front of her. The room was quiet, save for the faint hum of the heater and the rhythmic tapping of her fingers against the keyboard.

She had landed a freelance interior design job for a small gallery in Montmartre. It wasn't much, but it was enough to pay her bills while she searched for something more permanent. The project gave her a sliver of hope—proof that she could rebuild her life.

Her phone buzzed beside her, pulling her attention from her work. She glanced at the screen and froze.

The message was from an unknown number.

"Running from me doesn't mean you're free. You'll always belong to me, Elena."

Her chest tightened, and her hands began to shake. She deleted the message immediately, as though that would erase the feeling of Luca's shadow looming over her.

She stood and paced the room, her thoughts spiraling. *How did he get my number? How does he always find me?*

Elena tried to push the fear aside, focusing on her work. But hours later, when she checked her email, her heart sank.

There was a message from the gallery owner, short and formal.

"Thank you for your submission. However, due to unforeseen circumstances, we will no longer be moving forward with your services. Payment for completed work will be processed."

Elena stared at the screen, her mind racing. She picked up the phone and called the gallery, her fingers trembling as she dialed.

The owner, a polite but distant woman, answered after a few rings. "Ah, Miss Rossi," she said, her tone hesitant. "I... I'm afraid the decision is final."

"But why?" Elena asked, trying to keep the desperation out of her voice. "I submitted everything you asked for. You were happy with my designs."

"Yes, we were," the woman admitted. "But... someone contacted us with concerns about your, er, background. It was unsettling."

Elena's stomach dropped. "Who?" she demanded.

"I'm sorry, Miss Rossi. I can't disclose that information," the woman said, her voice softening. "I wish you the best."

The call ended, leaving Elena staring at the phone in disbelief. She didn't need to ask who had done it.

It was Luca.

The rain had stopped by the time Elena left the apartment. She walked through the crowded streets of Paris, her mind clouded with frustration and fear. The city's charm, which had once been a comfort, now felt distant and uninviting.

As she turned a corner, heading toward a café she frequented, she noticed a figure leaning casually against a lamppost.

For a moment, her heart seized.

But as she drew closer, she recognized him. Dominic Moreau.

He was dressed in a tailored black overcoat, his hands in his pockets, his gaze fixed on the street ahead. His presence was magnetic, drawing the attention of passersby without him even trying.

Elena hesitated, unsure whether to approach him or continue walking. But before she could decide, he turned his head and saw her.

"Miss Rossi," he said, his voice smooth and composed.

She stopped in her tracks. "You..."

Dominic pushed off the lamppost and stepped toward her, his movements deliberate and unhurried. "You look like someone who could use a strong cup of coffee," he remarked, his gray eyes scanning her face.

Elena blinked, unsure how to respond. It wasn't a question, and yet she felt compelled to follow him.

"Come," he said simply, nodding toward the café across the street.

THE CAFÉ SCENE

The café was warm, filled with the comforting aroma of roasted coffee and freshly baked pastries. Dominic led her to a table near the window, where he removed his coat and draped it over the back of his chair with a precision that felt almost rehearsed.

Elena sat opposite him, feeling suddenly out of place. He seemed perfectly at ease, his sharp features softened by the golden light filtering through the window.

"Have you settled into Paris?" Dominic asked as he gestured for a waiter.

Elena hesitated. "I'm... trying."

His gaze sharpened, though his expression remained neutral. "Trying is better than giving up," he said.

The waiter arrived, and Dominic ordered without looking at the menu—an espresso for himself and a café au lait for Elena.

"How do you know what I want?" she asked, her brow furrowing.

He smirked faintly. "A guess," he said.

Silence hung between them as they waited for the drinks. Elena felt the weight of his presence, the way he seemed to take up more space than he should. She fidgeted with the edge of her scarf, unsure what to say.

"You seem... troubled," Dominic said finally, breaking the silence.

She looked up, startled. "I—no, I'm fine."

He tilted his head slightly, as if assessing her. "You don't lie very convincingly, Miss Rossi."

Her cheeks flushed. She opened her mouth to protest, but the arrival of their drinks interrupted her.

Dominic lifted his espresso cup, his movements precise, deliberate. "Whatever it is, I imagine you'll find a way through it," he said, his tone quiet but certain. "You strike me as someone who does not give up easily."

Elena stared at him, unsure whether his words were meant to reassure her or challenge her. Either way, they left her feeling exposed, as though he could see through the carefully constructed walls she had built around herself.

4: A Storm Brews

The streets of Paris were quiet that evening, the faint glow of streetlights reflecting off the damp cobblestones. Elena hurried back to her apartment, clutching her coat tightly around her as the wind whipped through the narrow streets.

Dominic's words replayed in her mind: "Sometimes the strongest thing you can do is ask for help."

The truth of it stung. She had always prided herself on being independent, even in the darkest days of her marriage. But Luca's shadow had grown larger with every step she'd taken to escape it.

When she reached her building, her steps faltered. The lights in the hallway flickered ominously, and a sense of unease settled over her. She shook it off, blaming her nerves, and made her way to the elevator.

The soft chime of her phone pulled her attention as she reached her door. She hesitated before unlocking it, glancing at the screen.

Another message from an unknown number.

"Do you really think you can run from me, Elena? You'll never be free."

Her fingers tightened around the phone as anger and fear mixed in her chest. She stepped into the apartment, locking the door behind her, and leaned against it for a moment. She closed her eyes and took a deep breath, willing herself to stay calm.

But calm was hard to come by when her phone buzzed again.

This time, the message came with a picture. It was her building, taken from across the street.

Elena's breath hitched.

He's here.

The Trap Tightens

Elena spent the next day looking over her shoulder, her nerves frayed by the constant feeling of being watched. She had thought Luca's reach would end once she left Milan, but his ability to find her seemed endless.

By evening, she had received a call from her landlady, Madame Berger. The older woman's tone was icy, her words curt.

"Miss Rossi," she began, "I'm afraid I have some troubling news."

"What is it?" Elena asked, dread pooling in her stomach.

"I've received a complaint about you from someone claiming to know you. He says you have a... troubled history. I cannot have troublemakers in my building, Miss Rossi."

Elena's mouth went dry. "That's not true! He's lying. Please, I—"

"I'm sorry," Madame Berger interrupted. "I've made up my mind. You'll need to vacate the apartment by the end of the week."

The line went dead.

Elena sank onto the couch, her head in her hands. First the job, and now this. Luca was methodical, cutting off every lifeline she had worked so hard to create.

DOMINIC'S INTERVENTION

The following evening, Elena wandered the city streets, unsure of where else to go. Her suitcase rolled behind her, its wheels clicking softly against the uneven pavement. She felt exposed and vulnerable, but her pride kept her from calling Sophia.

It was nearly midnight when she found herself sitting on a bench near the Seine, her arms wrapped around herself to keep warm. She stared at the dark water, her thoughts swirling.

A black car pulled up quietly at the curb, its headlights cutting through the fog.

Elena barely noticed it until the door opened and a familiar figure stepped out.

Dominic Moreau.

He approached her slowly, his coat billowing slightly in the breeze. His gray eyes were steady, but his expression carried a rare softness that caught her off guard.

"You look like you've had a long day, Miss Rossi," he said.

Elena laughed bitterly, the sound surprising even herself. "That's one way to put it," she said, her voice shaking.

Dominic glanced at her suitcase, then back at her. "What happened?"

Elena hesitated. Part of her wanted to keep her problems to herself, but the weight of it all threatened to crush her. She exhaled and told him everything—Luca's threats, the messages, the eviction.

Dominic listened without interrupting, his gaze fixed on her as she spoke. When she finished, she felt raw, exposed.

"Why didn't you tell someone sooner?" he asked quietly.

"I didn't think anyone could help," she admitted.

Dominic's jaw tightened. He reached into his coat pocket and pulled out a phone. "Consider that problem solved."

"What do you mean?" she asked, frowning.

"You'll see," he said simply, dialing a number.

Elena watched as he spoke briefly in French, his tone calm but firm. When he ended the call, he looked at her again.

"There's a place for you to stay. Somewhere safe."

Elena blinked, her mind racing. "But I can't afford—"

"It's taken care of," Dominic interrupted.

"Why are you doing this for me?" she asked, her voice barely above a whisper.

Dominic held her gaze for a moment before answering. "Because someone needs to."

5: The Confrontation

A Presence That Cannot Be Ignored

The knock at the door sent ice through Elena's veins.
It was late—too late for visitors.
She stood frozen in place, her breath shallow.
She didn't have to check. She knew who it was.
Luca.
Her fingers trembled as she reached for the lock—but before she could touch it, something shifted behind her.
A second presence. A change in the air.
Then—a voice.
"You should step away from the door, Miss Rossi."
Elena's breath hitched.
She turned slowly.
Dominic.
He stood in the dim light of the entryway, his coat draped over his arm, his sharp features unreadable. He hadn't knocked. He hadn't announced himself.
He had simply arrived.
His presence filled the room, effortless yet absolute.
"How did you—" she started, but the words faltered.
Dominic didn't answer. His gaze flickered to the door.
"Go sit down," he murmured.
Elena hesitated.
Then the knock came again—harder.
"Elena!"
She flinched.

But Dominic didn't.

Without another word, he stepped forward and unlocked the door.

The heavy wood swung open, revealing Luca.

His expression twisted from anger to confusion as he took in the man standing before him.

He hadn't expected Dominic Moreau.

For the first time, Luca hesitated.

Dominic tilted his head slightly, watching him with the slow patience of someone who already knew how this would end.

"You've come a long way," Dominic said smoothly. "To make a mistake."

Luca's jaw clenched. "This has nothing to do with you."

Dominic exhaled softly, as if disappointed. Then, with deliberate ease, he took one step forward.

Luca—without thinking—took a step back.

Dominic smiled. A slow, deliberate gesture. Not friendly. Not threatening. Just controlled.

"If you come near her again," Dominic murmured, "you won't get another warning."

Luca's fists tightened. His face burned with frustration, but something deeper flickered in his eyes.

Fear.

Then, without breaking eye contact, Dominic reached into his coat pocket.

He wasn't holding a weapon.

But Luca stiffened anyway.

The air stretched thin.

Then, with effortless precision, Dominic adjusted his cuff, as if Luca no longer interested him.

"I trust we won't see you again," he said smoothly.

Luca's mouth opened—then closed.

Something in his stance collapsed slightly.

And then, he left.

The door shut softly behind him.

Silence.

Elena's pulse thundered in her ears.

She turned to Dominic, her voice unsteady. "What... what did you do?"

Dominic's gaze flickered toward her.

"I simply reminded him," he said quietly, "who he was dealing with."

A shiver ran down her spine.

She wasn't afraid of Dominic Moreau.

But she was beginning to realize...

Luca was.

6: The Long Drive

The Walk Home & The Rolls-Royce

The night was colder than she expected.

Elena wrapped her coat tighter around herself as she stepped out of the café, her mind heavy with exhaustion.

Her inbox was full of rejections.

Her bank account was running dangerously low.

She had been in Paris for weeks, but it felt like the city was pushing her out.

She sighed, adjusting the strap of her bag. She had no choice but to walk back to the townhouse—she couldn't afford unnecessary taxis anymore.

The streets were quieter now, the distant hum of traffic the only sound as she crossed onto a dimly lit avenue.

Then—she heard it.

A deep, smooth purr.

Not footsteps.

Not voices.

An engine.

Elena's breath caught as a black Rolls-Royce Phantom pulled up beside her, its presence so seamless that she hadn't even noticed its approach.

It didn't rush.

It didn't call for her.

It just arrived.

As if it had always been there.

The moment the car settled, the rear door opened automatically—smooth, silent, expectant.

No voice greeted her.

No explanation was given.

But he was inside.

Elena's fingers tightened around the strap of her bag.

She knew she should keep walking.

She should ignore the car, ignore the man inside it, ignore the way he seemed to appear whenever she tried to regain control of her own life.

And yet—

The night felt heavier than before.

Her world felt too large.

And he was the only thing that made sense.

Without a word, Elena stepped forward and got in.

THE DRIVE

The city passed in a blur outside the window.

Neither of them spoke.

The silence wasn't awkward. It was charged.

Elena stole a glance at Mr. Moreau.

One hand rested on the steering wheel, the other against the car's center console. He drove with the same precise ease he carried everywhere.

He wasn't watching her.

But he knew she was watching him.

She looked away first.

At some point, the car slowed.

They were on the outskirts of the city now, near a stretch of open road lined with trees.

The hum of the engine was the only sound between them.

Elena turned slightly. "Why?"

Dominic exhaled, tapping his fingers once against the wheel.

Then, finally, he looked at her.

"Why what?"

She swallowed. "Why did you stop?"

He was quiet for a long moment.

Then, instead of answering, he reached into his coat pocket and pulled out a cigarette.

He lit it with practiced ease, the orange glow momentarily illuminating his sharp features before he exhaled a slow spiral of smoke into the night.

He didn't offer her one.

He didn't speak.

He simply existed, unbothered, unwavering.

The world outside was dark, endless.

And for the first time in a long time, Elena didn't feel alone.

A PRESENCE THAT WOULDN'T Leave

Elena walked back toward her apartment, her hands shoved into her coat pockets.

The wind cut through her, but it wasn't just the cold that made her shiver.

It was the feeling of being watched.

She had sensed it all day—subtle, just beyond her reach. A shadow she couldn't shake.

Her fingers tightened.

She refused to turn around. She wouldn't give Luca the satisfaction of knowing he was getting to her.

Her apartment building was only two blocks away.

Just keep walking.

One block.

The feeling grew stronger.

Half a block.

Her breathing quickened.

Then—a hand closed around her wrist.

"Elena."

Her body froze.

Luca.

She wrenched her arm back, but his grip was iron.

"You've been ignoring me," he said, his voice quiet—but not soft. "That's not very kind."

Elena swallowed hard, trying to stay calm. "Let go of me."

But Luca just smiled. "You always had such a sharp tongue." His fingers tightened, pulling her closer. "It's adorable, really."

Her pulse pounded. Pedestrians passed them, oblivious. To everyone else, he looked like a man talking to his lover.

But Elena could feel the pressure behind his grip.

And she knew—he was done playing.

"I told you to let go," she said, her voice sharper this time.

Luca leaned in, his lips dangerously close to her ear.

"And I told you," he whispered, "you'll never be free of me."

She shoved against his chest—hard.

The sudden movement made him stumble back a step, his grip loosening for a fraction of a second.

It was all she needed.

Elena ripped her wrist free and took a step back, her breath ragged.

People were staring now.

Luca's expression twisted, something dark and furious flickering behind his polished facade.

"Elena," he said slowly, his voice losing its charm, "don't make me—"

A shadow passed between them.

A barrier.

A man.

A presence so overwhelming that even Luca froze.

Elena's breath caught.

Dominic.

He hadn't spoken. Hadn't needed to.

He had simply appeared.

Luca's fingers twitched at his sides, his confidence wavering.

For a long moment, no one spoke.

Then, finally, Dominic tilted his head slightly.

"Walk away," he said, his voice low, smooth. "While you still can."

The street seemed smaller.

Luca swallowed, but his pride kept him standing. "You don't scare me, Moreau."

Dominic's lips curved into a slow, dangerous smirk.

"That's your first mistake."

Luca inhaled sharply.

Then—he left.

The second he disappeared around the corner, Elena exhaled the breath she hadn't realized she'd been holding.

The city felt larger again.

She turned to Dominic, her throat dry.

"How do you always know where I am?" she asked, not sure if she wanted the answer.

Dominic didn't look at her immediately.

Instead, he reached into his coat pocket, pulled out a cigarette, and lit it with practiced ease.

Only after he exhaled did he speak.

"You should be asking," he murmured, his voice unreadable, "why he hasn't learned his lesson yet."

Elena stared at him.

A quiet chill ran down her spine.

Because Dominic hadn't been protecting her.

He had been waiting.
For Luca to cross the line.
And now, she realized—Luca just had.

7: The Grip of the Past

The weight of exhaustion pressed against Elena's chest as she scrolled through yet another rejection email.

She sat in a small rented workspace, her laptop open, her coffee untouched. The city bustled outside, but inside, her world was shrinking.

Every attempt to rebuild her life was being systematically destroyed.

She had applied for twelve jobs in the past two weeks.

All had responded with polite rejections.

Or worse—silence.

At first, she thought it was bad luck.

Then, she heard the whispers.

"She's unstable. Not reliable."

"She left something behind in Milan."

"A woman like that... too much drama."

Luca.

He wasn't just haunting her. He was erasing her.

A chill crept up her spine as she closed her laptop.

Her heart pounded as she realized:

If she couldn't work, she couldn't stay.

And if she couldn't stay... she had nowhere else to go.

A PRESENCE THAT WOULDN'T Leave

Elena walked back toward her apartment, her hands shoved into her coat pockets.

The wind cut through her, but it wasn't just the cold that made her shiver.

It was the feeling of being watched.

She had sensed it all day—subtle, just beyond her reach. A shadow she couldn't shake.

Her fingers tightened.

She refused to turn around. She wouldn't give Luca the satisfaction of knowing he was getting to her.

Her apartment building was only two blocks away.

Just keep walking.

One block.

The feeling grew stronger.

Half a block.

Her breathing quickened.

Then—a hand closed around her wrist.

"Elena."

Her body froze.

Luca.

She wrenched her arm back, but his grip was iron.

"You've been ignoring me," he said, his voice quiet—but not soft. "That's not very kind."

Elena swallowed hard, trying to stay calm. "Let go of me."

But Luca just smiled. "You always had such a sharp tongue." His fingers tightened, pulling her closer. "It's adorable, really."

Her pulse pounded. Pedestrians passed them, oblivious. To everyone else, he looked like a man talking to his lover.

But Elena could feel the pressure behind his grip.

And she knew—he was done playing.

"I told you to let go," she said, her voice sharper this time.

Luca leaned in, his lips dangerously close to her ear.

"And I told you," he whispered, "you'll never be free of me."

She shoved against his chest—hard.

The sudden movement made him stumble back a step, his grip loosening for a fraction of a second.

It was all she needed.

Elena ripped her wrist free and took a step back, her breath ragged.

People were staring now.

Luca's expression twisted, something dark and furious flickering behind his polished facade.

"Elena," he said slowly, his voice losing its charm, "don't make me—"

A shadow passed between them.

A barrier.

A man.

A presence so overwhelming that even Luca froze.

Elena's breath caught.

Dominic.

He hadn't spoken. Hadn't needed to.

He had simply appeared.

Luca's fingers twitched at his sides, his confidence wavering.

For a long moment, no one spoke.

Then, finally, Dominic tilted his head slightly.

"Walk away," he said, his voice low, smooth. "While you still can."

The street seemed smaller.

Luca swallowed, but his pride kept him standing. "You don't scare me, Moreau."

Dominic's lips curved into a slow, dangerous smirk.

"That's your first mistake."

Luca inhaled sharply.

Then—he left.

The second he disappeared around the corner, Elena exhaled the breath she hadn't realized she'd been holding.

The city felt larger again.

She turned to Dominic, her throat dry.

"How do you always know where I am?" she asked, not sure if she wanted the answer.

Dominic didn't look at her immediately.

Instead, he reached into his coat pocket, pulled out a cigarette, and lit it with practiced ease.

Only after he exhaled did he speak.

"You should be asking," he murmured, his voice unreadable, "why he hasn't learned his lesson yet."

Elena stared at him.

A quiet chill ran down her spine.

Because Dominic hadn't been protecting her.

He had been waiting.

For Luca to cross the line.

And now, she realized—Luca just had.

8: A Silent Warning

The city felt colder than before.

Elena walked quickly, her coat pulled tightly around her. Her wrist still ached where Luca had grabbed her.

His voice still rang in her ears.

"You'll never be free of me."

The words had coiled around her like chains.

But the moment he had seen him—he had let go.

The shift had been instant. The moment Dominic had stepped forward, Luca had retreated.

He hadn't fought.

He had run.

And that terrified her more than anything.

THE CAR THAT WAS ALWAYS There

She turned the corner onto a quieter street.

The night air was still. Too still.

Then—headlights swept over her.

Slow. Measured. Deliberate.

A black Rolls-Royce pulled smoothly up beside her, its presence as quiet as it was absolute.

The rear door opened automatically.

No invitation. No words.

Just Dominic.

Seated inside. Waiting.

Elena stopped walking, her breath unsteady.

She had two choices.
Walk away.
Or get in.
Her fingers tightened around the strap of her bag.
She exhaled.
And stepped inside.

THE DRIVE IN SILENCE

The city passed in a blur.

Elena kept her gaze on the window, but she could feel him beside her.

Still. Unshaken.

Like nothing had happened.

Like he hadn't just unraveled Luca without saying a single word.

The only sound in the car was the soft hum of the engine.

Finally, she glanced at him.

His expression was unreadable.

But his watch was missing.

Her breath caught.

She looked at his wrist—his sleeves were pulled back slightly. The skin there was bare.

That watch had been on his wrist earlier.

Now, it was gone.

Her fingers curled. What had he done?

THE WARNING THAT WAS Never Spoken

When the car pulled up to her apartment, Elena hesitated.

Dominic didn't move. Didn't look at her.

Didn't explain.

He simply reached into his coat pocket.

Pulled out a cigarette.
Lit it with the same practiced ease.
Then exhaled, sending a slow spiral of smoke curling into the night.
His watch was still missing.
Elena's pulse pounded.
Luca had run.
And now—something told her he wouldn't be coming back.
She swallowed hard, gripping the door handle.
She stepped out onto the sidewalk.
Dominic still didn't speak.
He just watched.
And in the silence, Elena understood.

9: No More Battles to Fight

The first thing Elena noticed was the silence.
Two days had passed since that night.
Since Dominic had driven her home. Since his watch had disappeared.
Since Luca had vanished.
Not a single call. Not a single message.
Nothing.
Her apartment had always felt small, but now it felt… empty.
Like something had been removed.
Like something had been cleaned up.
She should have felt safe.
She didn't.

SOMETHING WAS WRONG

Elena sat at a café, stirring her coffee absently.
She hadn't planned to come here. She had meant to stay home, keep searching for jobs, try to rebuild the pieces of her life.
But something had pulled her outside.
The feeling.
The nagging feeling that something was off.
She hadn't heard from Luca. She hadn't even seen him.
No texts. No more whispers at job interviews. No sudden encounters.
Nothing.
Like he had never existed.

She pulled out her phone, her fingers hesitating over his name.

Then—she heard them.

Two men at a nearby table. Talking.

"...Moretti's done."

Elena stilled.

"Gone?" one man asked. "Just like that?"

"Not just gone. Ruined." A quiet chuckle. "You know what happens when someone crosses Moreau."

Elena's blood ran cold.

Dominic.

THE CONFIRMATION SHE Didn't Want

She forced herself to breathe, forced herself to sit still, forced herself not to react.

She didn't know these men. But they knew Dominic.

And they knew what he had done.

One of them shook his head. "I told Moretti he was playing with fire. He should have walked away the first time."

The other man hummed. "Not like he had a choice in the end."

A quiet laugh. "No one does."

Elena's fingers tightened around her coffee cup.

This wasn't a coincidence.

Luca hadn't just backed down.

He had been taken down.

And now, he was gone.

Her stomach twisted.

She had wanted Luca gone. She had wanted to be free.

But not like this.

Not like Dominic Moreau had just erased him from existence.

THE PRESENCE THAT WAS Always There

Elena stood abruptly, grabbing her bag and stepping outside.
The air was cool against her flushed skin.
She needed to think.
She needed space.
She needed—
A black Rolls-Royce pulled up beside her.
Smooth. Effortless. Like it had always been waiting.
The door opened automatically.
No invitation.
No voice calling her name.
Just Dominic.
Seated inside. Silent. Watching.
Elena stared at him, her pulse thrumming in her ears.
A choice.
Again.
Her fingers curled into fists.
Then, slowly, she got in.

THE UNSPOKEN TRUTH

The car pulled away.
Neither of them spoke.
Elena turned toward him, studying his profile. Sharp. Untouched. Unbothered.
Like he hadn't just erased a man from her life.
Like he hadn't just ended something she didn't even understand.
She exhaled sharply, looking away. "He's gone."
Dominic didn't react. Didn't even blink.
But something in the air shifted.
She turned back to him. "You did something."
Still—silence.

She could feel her pulse in her throat. "What happened to him?"

Dominic finally looked at her.

And smirked.

Nothing else.

Just a slow, effortless smirk.

Like she already knew the answer.

Like he didn't have to say a word.

Elena's breath caught.

And for the first time…

She realized she wasn't afraid of Luca anymore.

She was afraid of him.

10: A Step Too Far

The days passed in silence.
Elena didn't reach out to Luca.
But he didn't reach out to her either.
There were no more whispered rumors at job interviews.
No more messages.
No more sudden encounters.
It was as if he had never existed.
And yet, Elena couldn't stop thinking about him.
Not Luca.
Dominic.
The way he had sat in that car, silent, unbothered. The way he had looked at her, smirked—like he knew exactly what she had realized.
Like he had known all along.
She had thought he was just a man with power.
But now?
Now, she understood.
He didn't just have power. He was power.

THE JOB THAT WAS NEVER Hers

Elena sat across from the director of a luxury interior design firm.
It was her fifth interview in two weeks.
And unlike the others, this one felt different.
The woman in front of her was polite, engaged. She listened, asked the right questions. She was interested.
For the first time, Elena felt a flicker of hope.

This could be it.

Then—the shift.

It was subtle. Barely noticeable.

A sudden stiffness in the woman's posture. The way her eyes flicked down to her phone screen for half a second.

Elena knew before she even heard the words.

"I'm sorry, Miss Rossi," the woman said, her tone cooling. "But the position has already been filled."

The air left Elena's lungs.

Not again.

Not when she had been so close.

She managed a nod, hiding the sting behind a polite smile. "Of course. Thank you for your time."

She walked out of the office, back onto the busy Parisian streets, her heartbeat pounding in her ears.

Someone had stopped this job from happening.

Someone had stepped in. Again.

And there was only one person who could do that.

THE CONFRONTATION THAT Never Happened

Elena stormed into the lobby of an exclusive five-star hotel.

She didn't know how she knew he would be here.

She just knew.

The receptionist barely had time to ask for her name before a quiet voice interrupted.

"Miss Rossi."

Elena turned.

And there he was.

Dominic Moreau.

Standing at the top of the marble staircase, dressed in an impossibly tailored black suit.

His presence was effortless.

He didn't react to her frustration. Didn't acknowledge the fire in her eyes.

He simply descended the stairs slowly, his hands in his pockets, his expression unreadable.

And with each step, her anger burned a little less.

Because how could she fight against something she couldn't even touch?

By the time he reached her, her breath had steadied.

But her heart had not.

She lifted her chin. "You did it."

Dominic didn't respond.

She inhaled sharply. "I had the job. I saw it in her eyes. And then—"

She stopped, searching his face.

But Dominic Moreau was unreadable.

He said nothing. He did nothing.

And yet, the truth was already there.

He had done it.

THE ANSWER THAT WAS Never Spoken

She exhaled. "Why?"

Silence.

Elena's pulse thundered in her ears.

Her voice lowered. "Why won't you let me work?"

Dominic's gaze flickered over her face, calm, composed.

Then, finally—he spoke.

Low. Measured.

"You think I kept you from working?"

She swallowed. "I don't think. I know."

A pause.

Then—a shift.

Dominic took a step forward.

Elena didn't move.

"You're looking in the wrong place, Miss Rossi," he murmured.

The words sent a quiet chill through her.

Her brow furrowed. "What does that mean?"

Dominic didn't answer.

He simply slipped something into her hand.

Something cold. Small.

She looked down.

A key.

Her breath caught. "What is this?"

Dominic exhaled a slow breath, stepping past her as he adjusted his cuff.

Then—he was gone.

Leaving Elena standing alone in the middle of the hotel lobby.

With a key she didn't ask for.

And an answer that had never been spoken.

11: The Door That Shouldn't Open

E lena turned the small, silver key over in her hands.
It was cold. Weightless. A promise she never asked for.
She sat at her kitchen table, staring at it, waiting for it to tell her something.
It didn't belong to her apartment.
She had tried. Twice.
Then she had tried the mailbox downstairs.
Nothing.
She had searched for any markings, anything that could tell her where it belonged. But there was nothing.
Just a key.
A key she never wanted.
A key she couldn't ignore.

THE SEARCH

The next morning, she walked through the city, the key hidden in her coat pocket.
She shouldn't have kept it.
She should have thrown it away.
But something wouldn't let her.
Her feet carried her without direction. Past the cafés, the boutiques, the winding Parisian streets.
Until—
She saw it.
A door.

Tall. Black. Ornate.
Elena didn't know why she stopped in front of it.
Didn't know why her hand trembled as she reached into her coat.
But she did.
And when she pulled out the key—her breath caught.
Because it matched.

THE LOCK THAT TURNED Too Easily
Elena hesitated.
The street was quiet. No one watching.
No one waiting.
Except the door itself.
She swallowed.
Then—she turned the key.
The lock clicked open effortlessly.
The door swung inward.
No resistance. No creak.
As if it had been waiting for her.
Elena stepped inside.

THE APARTMENT SHE NEVER Asked For
She exhaled sharply.
It wasn't a hotel room.
It wasn't an office.
It was an apartment.
A penthouse.
Expansive. Breathtaking.
It was hers.
Or rather—
It had been given to her.

By him.

She stood in the middle of the silent space, her heart hammering against her ribs.

The living room stretched out in front of her, a floor-to-ceiling window revealing a breathtaking view of the city.

Everything was untouched.

As if no one had ever lived here.

Or as if someone had been waiting for her to arrive.

Elena's hands curled into fists.

This wasn't a mistake.

This wasn't a coincidence.

This was Dominic.

And this time, he wasn't just watching.

He was giving.

Without asking.

Without explaining.

Without permission.

THE PRESENCE THAT WAS Always There

She turned sharply, her breath uneven.

She expected him to be there.

Watching. Waiting. Silent.

But the doorway was empty.

The room was empty.

And yet—

he was still there.

Not physically. Not in sight.

But in everything.

In the pristine, untouched furniture.

In the view of the city that stretched before her.

In the key that still sat, cold and weightless, in her palm.

He had done this.
And he had left her to decide.

12: The Choice She Didn't Make

The apartment was too quiet.

Elena paced the living room, her footsteps muffled by the thick, luxurious carpet. Sunlight streamed through the massive windows, painting the walls in warm golds and soft shadows.

But all she could feel was the weight of his presence in every corner.

Dominic Moreau.

She gripped the key in her hand, its sharp edges pressing into her palm.

She should leave. She should turn around, walk out, and never come back.

But she didn't.

Because despite everything—despite the uncertainty, the questions, the unease—she felt a pull.

A pull toward him.

Toward the world he was offering, without words, without explanation.

She sank onto the sleek leather couch, her gaze drifting over the untouched space. Everything here was perfect. Immaculate. As if waiting for her to breathe life into it.

But it wasn't hers.

And that made all the difference.

SEARCHING FOR ANSWERS

She spent the next few days alternating between her cramped apartment and the penthouse.

She searched for clues. A note, a sign, something that would explain why.

But there was nothing.

No messages. No appearances.

Just silence.

It was maddening.

Elena found herself lingering by the windows, watching the city move beneath her, waiting for a glimpse of the black Rolls-Royce.

But it never came.

Dominic was nowhere.

And yet, he was everywhere.

AN UNEXPECTED ARRIVAL

On the third evening, as dusk settled over Paris, a soft knock echoed through the penthouse.

Elena's heart leapt into her throat.

She crossed the room cautiously, her bare feet silent against the floor.

When she opened the door, her breath caught.

Dominic.

He stood in the doorway, his dark coat draped over his arm, his expression as unreadable as ever.

For a moment, neither of them spoke.

Then, with the faintest hint of a smile, he stepped inside, closing the door softly behind him.

Elena's pulse raced. She hadn't expected him to come here. Hadn't expected him to enter her space—this space.

She found her voice. "Why did you give me this?"

Dominic glanced around the apartment, his gaze lingering on the view through the windows. "I thought it would suit you."

THE SILENT OATH

She frowned, frustration bubbling beneath her calm facade. "I didn't ask for this."

His eyes flicked to hers, sharp, assessing. "No. You didn't."

Silence stretched between them. Heavy. Unspoken.

Elena exhaled, her fingers twisting the key still clutched in her hand. "You're playing games with me."

Dominic tilted his head slightly, a shadow of amusement flickering across his face. "Am I?"

She stepped forward, her voice firmer. "You controlled everything. My job, my apartment—now this. What do you want from me?"

Dominic's gaze softened, just a fraction.

Then, in a move so subtle she almost missed it, he reached out and gently took the key from her hand.

For a heartbeat, their fingers touched. Warmth spread through her, unexpected and unwelcome.

Dominic looked down at the key, turning it between his fingers. "You're free to leave, Miss Rossi. Anytime you wish."

She stared at him, her breath shallow. "But you know I won't."

His lips curved into a small, knowing smile. "I know you'll make the choice that's right for you."

Elena's jaw tightened. She didn't like the feeling of being maneuvered, of being cornered into decisions she didn't understand.

But the truth was—he was right.

She couldn't walk away.

Not yet.

An Unspoken Agreement

Dominic placed the key on the table between them, his gaze never leaving hers.

"You asked me what I want," he said quietly. "I want you to see beyond what's in front of you."

Elena frowned. "What does that mean?"

He didn't answer.

Instead, he turned, his coat draped over his arm, and moved toward the door.

Before he left, he glanced back at her, his expression softer than she'd ever seen it.

"Lock the door when you leave," he murmured. "Or when you decide to stay."

Then he was gone.

Leaving her alone in the silence once more.

But this time, the silence felt different.

Less like emptiness.

And more like possibility.

13: The Shadows That Follow

The apartment no longer felt like a stranger's.

Elena told herself she was just staying for the night. Just testing the waters. Just trying to understand why Dominic had done this.

But deep down, she knew the truth.

She had already chosen to stay.

She walked through the penthouse, running her fingers lightly over the smooth marble counters, the carefully curated books on the shelves. The place was furnished, but it didn't feel lived in.

It felt prepared.

For her.

THE PIECES THAT DIDN'T Fit

She found herself in the bedroom, standing in front of a dark wooden wardrobe.

It should have been empty.

But when she pulled it open, she froze.

Inside, neatly arranged, were her clothes.

The same items from her previous apartment, folded to perfection.

Her breath caught. She turned, opening the dresser.

More of her belongings.

The small silver bracelet she thought she had lost. Her favorite book, the worn pages soft from years of turning.

It was all here.

Moved. Placed.

Prepared.
She exhaled, trying to steady herself.
She should have been unnerved.
But instead—her heart ached.
Because this wasn't just control.
This was care.
And that was more dangerous than anything.

A CALL THAT CHANGED Everything

Her phone buzzed, jolting her from her thoughts.
An unknown number.
She hesitated before answering.
"Elena Rossi."
A pause. Then—a man's voice. Low. Cold. Unfamiliar.
"You should leave while you still can."
The blood drained from her face. "Who is this?"
Silence.
Then—a quiet chuckle.
"Tell Moreau he's losing control."
The line went dead.
Elena's heart slammed against her ribs.
She pulled the phone away, her hands shaking.
This wasn't about her.
This was about Dominic.
And whoever this man was—he wasn't afraid of him.

A PRESENCE THAT WAS Always There

The knock at the door wasn't loud.
But it still sent a sharp jolt through her.

She turned slowly.

For a long moment, she just stood there, staring.

Then, with unsteady fingers, she unlocked the door and pulled it open.

And there he was.

Dominic Moreau.

Standing in the hallway, coat unbuttoned, tie loosened, his sharp gray eyes taking in every detail of her expression.

He had known.

Somehow, he had already known.

Without thinking, Elena whispered, "Someone called me."

His gaze darkened.

She swallowed. "They said you're losing control."

A long silence.

Then, Dominic stepped inside.

And for the first time, Elena felt like she wasn't the one being hunted.

She wasn't the target.

He was.

14: The War She Never Saw

Dominic stepped inside without hesitation.

Elena barely moved as he brushed past her, his presence shifting the air in the room.

He didn't ask questions. Didn't demand answers.

Because he already knew.

She closed the door slowly, her fingers trembling slightly. "Are you going to tell me what's going on?"

Dominic shrugged off his coat, draping it over the back of a chair. He didn't look at her immediately. Instead, he took in the space, his gaze assessing, searching.

Like he was looking for something she couldn't see.

Finally, he spoke. "What exactly did they say?"

Elena swallowed. "Someone called me."

His expression remained unreadable.

"They told me to leave."

His jaw tightened, but he didn't react.

Her pulse quickened. "And... they said you're losing control."

A pause.

Then—the faintest hint of amusement flickered in his eyes.

Like it was almost funny.

Like the idea of Dominic Moreau losing control was so far from reality that it was laughable.

But Elena didn't laugh.

Because whoever had called her wasn't joking.

And Dominic wasn't denying it.

THE SHIFT IN POWER

He turned to her, finally meeting her gaze. "Did they mention a name?"

"No."

"Accent?"

She hesitated. "French. But… I don't know if that means anything."

Dominic nodded slightly, as if filing the information away.

Elena frowned. "You're not surprised."

He tilted his head. "Should I be?"

She exhaled sharply. "Someone just called me to threaten you, and you're acting like it's just another Tuesday."

Dominic smirked faintly. "It is."

The response sent a chill through her.

Because he wasn't being arrogant.

He was being honest.

This wasn't new to him.

And that terrified her more than anything.

A GAME SHE NEVER KNEW She Was Playing

Elena turned away, running a hand through her hair.

"I don't understand any of this," she admitted. "Why me? Why did they call me?"

Dominic watched her for a moment before stepping forward.

Slowly. Deliberately.

He stopped just close enough for her to feel the warmth of his presence.

Then, in a voice so quiet it was almost dangerous, he said—"Because they think you matter."

Her breath caught.

She looked up at him, her pulse hammering.

His gaze was unreadable. Calm. Absolute.

Like he had already decided something.
Like he had already chosen.
And so had she.

THE FIRST REAL THREAT

A sharp knock shattered the moment.

Elena stiffened.

Dominic didn't move.

He glanced toward the door, his expression smooth, but his body shifted.

Subtle. Controlled.

Like he was ready.

Elena swallowed. "Are you expecting someone?"

Dominic didn't answer.

Instead, he stepped past her, his fingers grazing her wrist for a fraction of a second. A silent order.

Stay back.

Then—he opened the door.

A man stood on the threshold.

Older. Refined. But dangerous in a way that wasn't immediately visible.

His sharp eyes flicked from Dominic to Elena, his lips curving slightly.

Then, he spoke.

"Moreau," he greeted smoothly. "I was beginning to think you were avoiding me."

Dominic didn't react.

He simply exhaled, slow and unbothered. "You've mistaken me for someone with time to waste."

Elena barely breathed.

Because this wasn't like Luca.

THE SILENT OATH

This wasn't someone who feared Dominic.
This was someone who saw him as an equal.
And that meant he was even more dangerous.

15: The Man Who Didn't Fear Him

Elena didn't move.

The air in the penthouse had shifted, thick with something unspoken, dangerous.

Dominic stood in front of her, his stance calm, measured.

But she could feel it.

The quiet tension in his body.

The way his fingers flexed slightly at his sides.

Like he was waiting.

Like he was deciding.

The man at the door was older, dressed in a perfectly tailored suit, his presence deliberate.

He looked at Dominic with something close to amusement.

Like he was entertained.

Like he knew exactly what buttons to push.

Elena swallowed, forcing herself to step closer. "Who is he?"

Dominic didn't look at her.

But his voice was smooth, steady. "Someone who wasn't invited."

The man smiled. "Now, that's not very welcoming."

Dominic exhaled slowly. "You were never welcome, Laurent."

THE FIRST CRACK IN the Surface

Victor Laurent.

The name meant nothing to Elena.

But the way Dominic said it—the weight behind it—made her chest tighten.

This wasn't business.

This was personal.

Victor's gaze shifted to her, slow and deliberate.

Elena's stomach twisted.

She didn't like the way he looked at her.

Not with interest. Not even with threat.

With understanding.

Like he already knew why she was here.

Like he knew exactly what Dominic had done to bring her into his world.

A slow smirk pulled at Victor's lips.

"I see now," he murmured.

Dominic's jaw tightened.

And just like that—the energy in the room shifted.

Not from Victor.

From Dominic.

Like he was done.

Like this game—whatever it was—had just reached its limit.

The Warning That Wasn't Spoken

Elena barely had time to blink before Dominic moved.
He didn't lunge. Didn't attack.
He simply took one measured step forward.
And Victor—laughed.
Low. Amused.
Like he had expected it.
Like he was enjoying it.
But he didn't move.
And Dominic didn't stop.
The space between them disappeared in an instant, the air thick, suffocating.
Elena's heart pounded.
She had never seen Dominic like this.
Not with Luca.
Not with anyone.
This wasn't the calm, effortless power he usually carried.
This was something darker.
More personal.
Victor tilted his head, voice smooth. "Careful, Moreau. You don't want her to see you like this, do you?"
Dominic's fingers twitched.
A single moment.
A single flicker of control almost slipping.
Elena felt it.
And so did Victor.
He smiled.
Then—he stepped back.
Not because he had to.
Because he had already won.
At least for now.

THE END OF A GAME SHE Didn't Know She Was In

Victor buttoned his jacket, glancing at Elena one last time.

"I imagine we'll be seeing more of each other," he said lightly. "I look forward to it."

Then, he turned and walked away.

No threats. No goodbyes.

Just a departure that felt like a promise.

The door clicked shut behind him.

And Dominic didn't move.

The Silence That Said Everything

Elena let out a shaky breath.

She turned to Dominic, searching his face.

His expression was unreadable.

But his fists were still clenched.

His body still wired.

And for the first time…

She wasn't sure if it was because of Victor.

Or because of her.

Because she had seen it.

The crack. The moment he had almost lost control.

And Dominic Moreau never lost control.

16: The Ghosts He Won't Name

The door had barely shut before Elena turned to Dominic.

The room still carried the weight of Victor Laurent's presence—like a shadow that refused to leave.

Dominic stood where he was, shoulders tense, hands at his sides.

He didn't move.

Didn't speak.

Elena's pulse hammered against her ribs. She had seen something different in him tonight. A crack in his control. A glimpse of something darker, colder.

And she wasn't sure if it was Victor who had caused it.

Or if it was her.

She swallowed, steadying her voice. "Who is he?"

Dominic exhaled slowly, then walked past her.

Not answering.

Not acknowledging.

Just moving.

Elena turned sharply, frustration rising. "Don't ignore me."

Dominic reached for his coat, adjusting the cuff of his sleeve with careful precision.

And then, without looking at her, he said—"Go to bed, Miss Rossi."

Her breath caught.

That was it?

He had stood toe-to-toe with a man who clearly held power over him, and now he was just—dismissing her?

Her fists clenched. "You think I can just pretend that didn't happen?"

Dominic finally met her gaze.

And for the first time—there was no amusement.

No unreadable smirk.

Just steel.

"This isn't your concern."

Her throat tightened. "He came to my door."

Dominic's gaze darkened.

Wrong move.

A BATTLE OF SILENCE

The tension between them shifted.

Elena felt the moment he made a decision.

A quiet resignation.

Then—he stepped toward her.

Slow. Measured.

She held her ground, pulse racing as he closed the space between them.

He didn't touch her.

Didn't reach for her.

But he was too close.

Close enough that the air between them felt heavy.

Close enough that she could feel the heat of him.

Close enough that she realized—she wasn't afraid.

Not of him.

Not of this.

Not even of the power that radiated from him in waves.

Dominic studied her face, his voice quiet but firm. "You don't need to understand this."

Elena's chest tightened. "You don't get to decide that."

A pause.
Then, in a voice like silk over steel, he murmured—"Yes, I do."
Her stomach flipped.
Because he meant it.
Not as a warning. Not as a threat.
As a fact.

THE ANSWER SHE DIDN'T Expect

Elena exhaled sharply, willing herself to stay steady.
She didn't care how powerful he was. How dangerous he was.
She wasn't going to let him walk away from this.
She wasn't Luca.
She wasn't one of his business dealings.
She was Elena Rossi.
And he had brought her into this.
She lifted her chin. "You keep saying I don't need to know."
Dominic waited.
She took a breath. "Then tell me—what do I need?"
Something flickered in his gaze.
Something unreadable.
Then—he stepped back.
The distance between them returned.
The air shifted.
And his next words—they weren't what she expected.
"You need to stop asking questions you don't want answers to."
Her breath caught.
Dominic turned, reaching for his coat.
This time, he didn't tell her to go to bed.
He just left.

17: The Game She Wasn't Supposed to Play

Dominic was gone.

But his presence still lingered, woven into the silence of the apartment.

Elena stood in the same spot, her heart pounding against her ribs.

He walked away.

For the first time, he was the one who left first.

Not because he was dismissing her.

Not because he was in control.

But because for a fraction of a second—he wasn't.

And that unsettled her more than anything.

She inhaled deeply, turning toward the window. The city stretched out before her, endless and glittering.

She should let this go.

She should pretend Victor Laurent never came to her door. Pretend Dominic Moreau hadn't stood in front of her, muscles wound tight with something she couldn't name.

But she wasn't going to.

Because Dominic had just confirmed something without saying a word.

Victor wasn't just an enemy.

He was a threat.

And Dominic didn't have as much control over him as he wanted her to believe.

LOOKING FOR ANSWERS in the Wrong Places

Elena wasn't reckless.

She wasn't foolish.

But she was stubborn.

And Dominic had left her with too many questions.

She spent the next morning searching.

There wasn't much on Victor Laurent. Not in the places normal people looked.

But Elena wasn't searching for normal.

She found his name in financial records, business acquisitions, discreet dealings that never made headlines.

He was powerful. Connected. Untouchable in a way that made her stomach twist.

But what stood out the most—was the pattern.

Victor Laurent only appeared in places where Dominic Moreau's name had already been.

Elena exhaled, her fingers tightening around her phone.

This wasn't about money.

This wasn't about business.

This was something deeper.

And she had just made the mistake of pulling on a thread she wasn't ready for.

THE MESSAGE THAT WASN'T Meant for Her

She had just closed her laptop when her phone buzzed.

Unknown number.

Her stomach flipped.

She hesitated, then answered. "Hello?"

A pause. Then—a low, smooth voice.

"I told you to leave while you still could."

Elena's blood ran cold.

THE SILENT OATH

Her fingers tightened around the phone. "Who is this?"

A quiet chuckle.

"You already know."

Her breath came faster.

Victor Laurent.

A chair scraped softly against the floor on the other end of the call, like he was settling in. Comfortable. Like he had time.

"I have to admit, I underestimated you, Miss Rossi."

Elena stayed silent, pulse hammering in her ears.

"But now you're making mistakes."

Her mouth felt dry. "What do you want?"

"I want you to understand something." His voice remained perfectly calm. Too calm.

"You're not a player in this game. You're a piece on the board. And Moreau? He's losing his grip on you."

A slow exhale.

"So tell me, Miss Rossi—what happens when he lets go?"

The call ended.

Elena stood frozen, the phone still pressed to her ear.

The room felt colder.

Because Victor Laurent hadn't threatened her.

He hadn't needed to.

He had simply told her the truth.

And now, she didn't know which was more terrifying—the idea that Dominic was losing control... or the idea that Victor was right.

18: The Moment He Stops Waiting

Elena didn't tell Dominic about the call.

She told herself it was because she didn't want to drag him into this. That she could handle it. That Victor Laurent's words meant nothing.

But deep down, she knew the truth.

She didn't tell Dominic because she didn't know how he would react.

And that scared her more than Victor ever could.

A PRESENCE THAT COULDN'T Be Ignored

The next evening, Elena sat at a small café, hands wrapped around a cup of untouched coffee.

She had spent the entire day trying to distract herself.

Trying to convince herself that Victor had only been trying to get into her head.

But the unease wouldn't leave her.

She had almost forgotten how it felt—to constantly look over her shoulder, to wonder who was watching.

To feel like she didn't belong to herself anymore.

Then—she felt it.

A shift.

A presence.

She looked up.

And there, leaning against a sleek black car across the street, stood Dominic Moreau.

Watching her.
Waiting.
As if he had known exactly where she would be.
As if he had known exactly what she had done.

THE DRIVE THAT WASN'T a Request

Elena didn't hesitate this time.

She left her coffee untouched, walked straight across the street, and got into the car.

The door shut softly behind her.

Dominic slid in beside her, calm, unreadable.

The car pulled away, the hum of the engine the only sound between them.

Neither of them spoke.

Neither of them needed to.

Because Dominic wasn't waiting for answers.

He already knew.

THE QUESTION THAT WAS Never Asked

They drove through the city, the tension between them thick.

Finally, Dominic exhaled slowly, his fingers tapping against the wheel.

"You should have told me."

Elena's stomach twisted.

He wasn't asking.

He was stating a fact.

She swallowed. "It was just a call."

Dominic's grip on the wheel tightened.

"Was it?"

A shiver ran down her spine.
Because he already knew it wasn't.

THE FIRST REAL CONSEQUENCE

The car slowed to a stop in front of the penthouse.

But Dominic didn't move.

Neither did she.

The silence between them stretched, filled with all the things he wasn't saying.

Then, without warning, he turned toward her.

Slow. Deliberate.

And for the first time since the call, Elena realized she had made a mistake.

Because she had spent all this time trying to understand Victor Laurent.

When she should have been asking herself—

What happens when Dominic stops waiting?

His voice was quiet, but it carried the weight of something final.

"You don't handle Laurent, Elena."

She barely breathed. "Then who does?"

Dominic's expression didn't change.

But his answer did.

"I do."

Her stomach dropped.

Because this time, Dominic wasn't walking away.

This time, he was making a move.

And whatever happened next—there was no turning back.

19: The Moment He Strikes

Dominic didn't act on impulse.
He wasn't a man who warned before making a move. He wasn't someone who reacted—he calculated, decided, executed.

And by the time anyone realized what he had done, it was already over.

Victor Laurent had made a mistake.

And now, he was about to understand what it meant to stand against Dominic Moreau.

THE NIGHT THAT CHANGED Everything

Elena didn't know where they were going.

Dominic had barely spoken since they left the penthouse.

But he didn't need to.

Because Elena could feel it—the tension in his body, the quiet finality in his presence.

This wasn't just about Victor's call.

This was about Dominic refusing to let anyone touch what was his.

And for the first time, she wondered—

Was she his to protect? Or his to claim?

A MEETING THAT WASN'T a Request

The car came to a stop in front of an exclusive hotel, one of those places with no name on the door.

A place for men like Dominic Moreau.

Men like Victor Laurent.

Elena barely had time to process before the door opened, and Dominic was already moving.

No hesitation. No uncertainty.

She followed, heart pounding, barely able to keep up as he walked straight through the lobby, past the reception, and into a private elevator.

Dominic didn't need to check where he was going.

He already knew.

VICTOR LAURENT NEVER Saw It Coming

The elevator doors opened.

A private penthouse.

And in the center of the room—Victor Laurent.

Seated. Waiting.

But he wasn't relaxed.

Because he had heard the footsteps.

And when he looked up—his smirk faltered.

Dominic didn't stop walking.

Didn't pause.

Didn't give Victor a chance to speak.

He simply crossed the room in measured, precise steps—

And pulled out a chair across from him.

Victor exhaled slowly, recovering. His smirk returned, but it didn't reach his eyes.

"To what do I owe the pleasure, Moreau?"

Dominic leaned back slightly, adjusting his cuff.

The movement was casual.

But the energy in the room was not.

Elena stood near the doorway, her pulse hammering, watching as two men—two predators—assessed each other.

And then—Dominic spoke.

A single, quiet statement.

"You made a mistake."

THE SHIFT IN POWER

Victor exhaled, shaking his head. "Did I?"

Dominic's gaze didn't waver.

"You involved her."

A pause.

Then—a flicker of something in Victor's expression.

Not fear.

But realization.

Slowly, he leaned forward, resting his elbows on the table.

"Ah," he murmured, looking past Dominic to where Elena stood. "So that's what this is about."

Dominic's fingers tapped once against the armrest.

A slow, deliberate movement.

Elena felt the shift before she even understood it.

Victor's expression changed.

His amusement faded.

Because he had just realized something.

Dominic Moreau wasn't here to discuss.

He was here to end something.

And Victor was out of moves.

THE UNSPOKEN WARNING

The silence stretched, thick with finality.

Victor studied Dominic carefully. "You don't like to be challenged, do you?"

Dominic exhaled slowly.

A soft, dangerous breath.

"No," he murmured.

And then, he stood.

Elena's breath caught as **Victor followed instinctively—**like his body already knew what was happening.

But Dominic had already turned away.

Already decided this conversation was over.

Victor clenched his jaw. "This isn't finished."

Dominic reached for the door.

Then—he glanced back.

And in a voice so calm it was lethal, he said—

"It is for you."

Then he walked out.

Leaving Victor Laurent behind.

Leaving Elena speechless.

Leaving behind no question about who had won.

20: A Love That Needed No Words

The drive back to the penthouse was silent.

Not the kind of silence that carried tension or anger.

But something softer.

Something that didn't need words.

Elena sat beside Dominic, staring out the window as the city lights flickered past.

She should be questioning everything.

Should be demanding answers.

But for the first time—she didn't want them.

Because tonight, she had seen something that had nothing to do with power or control.

She had seen him.

Not the businessman. Not the untouchable Dominic Moreau.

But the man who had walked into a room and ended a war before it could start.

For her.

And he hadn't asked for anything in return.

A DIFFERENT KIND OF Quiet

The penthouse was dark when they stepped inside, the city lights spilling through the windows, casting long shadows across the floor.

Dominic placed his keys on the table, removed his coat, then exhaled slowly—as if releasing something only he could feel.

Elena watched him from across the room.

She should say something.

Should thank him.
Should ask why he had done it.
But she didn't.
Because deep down—she already knew.

A LOVE THAT EXISTED in Silence

He walked past her, heading toward the bar, but not to drink.
Instead, he reached for a glass, filled it with water, then turned—
And held it out to her.
Elena blinked.
She hadn't realized how dry her throat was.
She took the glass carefully, her fingers brushing his just for a second.
The touch sent something deep and aching through her chest.
Not desire. Not temptation.
Something far more dangerous.
Something real.
She swallowed and took a slow sip, never breaking eye contact.
Dominic said nothing.
But he didn't have to.
Because this wasn't a gesture of power.
This wasn't about control.
This was care.
And that was more intimate than anything else.

THE SPACE THAT NO LONGER Existed

Elena placed the glass down, her hands lingering against the counter.
Dominic stood a few feet away, his posture relaxed but his gaze soft.

Not unreadable.
Not closed off.
Just watching her.
Like she was the only thing that existed in this moment.
Her pulse stuttered.
He had never asked her to stay.
Never spoken the words.
But his presence had always pulled her back.
And now, she realized—
She had stopped resisting.

An Unspoken Promise

She inhaled shakily, finally finding her voice.
"Dominic."
His name tasted different on her tongue. Softer.
His expression didn't change, but she saw it—the small shift in his stance.
Like he had been waiting to hear her say it like that.
She wanted to say more.
Wanted to tell him that she understood.
That she wasn't afraid.
That whatever this was—it was real.
But she didn't have to.
Because Dominic reached past her—not to touch her, but to brush his fingers against the light switch.
The room dimmed into a soft golden glow, turning the world around them into something smaller, quieter.
A space where only they existed.
And in that moment, Elena understood.
This wasn't about power.
It was about a love that didn't need to be spoken.
Because it was already there.
In the way he waited for her to feel safe.

In the way he never pushed, never asked.
In the way he always knew what she needed—before she did.
Her heart ached with it.
Not with uncertainty.
Not with fear.
With the kind of love that every girl dreams of but never dares to believe is real.
And yet—here it was.
In the silence.
In the space between them.
In him.
Dominic Moreau.
The man who had never once said the words.
But had always, always made sure she felt them.

21: A Love That Needed No Permission

Elena didn't sleep that night.

She lay awake in the quiet of the penthouse, listening to the distant hum of the city, her heart full of something too big to name.

Dominic had never asked her to stay.

But he had never let her feel like she needed to leave, either.

He hadn't spoken of love.

Hadn't tried to define whatever this was.

But he had made sure she felt it.

And now, for the first time, she let herself believe it was real.

A MORNING THAT FELT Different

When Elena woke, the sunlight stretched softly across the room, casting golden hues over the elegant furniture.

The space felt lighter.

As if something between them had shifted.

She stepped out of the bedroom, her bare feet silent against the cool floor.

And then—she saw him.

Dominic stood by the window, dressed in a crisp white shirt, sleeves rolled up, coffee in hand.

The morning light kissed his sharp features, making him look less like the untouchable businessman she had first met, and more like the man she had come to know.

The one who waited.

The one who never asked, but always understood.

The one who had quietly built a place for her here—long before she realized she belonged.

THE GESTURE THAT SAID Everything

He turned when he sensed her, his gaze meeting hers.

A flicker of warmth passed through his expression—a look so subtle, yet so intimate, it stole her breath.

Elena hesitated, then walked toward him.

Neither of them spoke.

There was nothing to say.

Dominic simply lifted his hand, holding out his coffee without looking away from her.

An unspoken invitation.

A simple, effortless gesture.

But in that moment—it meant everything.

Elena took the cup from his hand, fingers brushing his for the briefest second.

Her heart ached with it.

Because this was love.

Not in grand declarations.

Not in whispered confessions.

But in small, quiet moments that didn't need words.

She took a slow sip, the warmth spreading through her chest.

Dominic didn't move, didn't press for anything.

He simply stood there, letting her come closer.

And Elena did.

Not because she had to.

Because she wanted to.

A LOVE THAT WAS ALWAYS There

She exhaled softly, setting the coffee down on the table beside them.

For a moment, she only watched him—the way the morning light played across his features, the way his presence filled the space around them without effort.

Dominic Moreau had never once tried to hold her back.

But somehow, he had become the place she always returned to.

A safe place.

A place she didn't want to leave.

And that—that was love.

Pure.

Steady.

Unshaken.

She didn't need to say it.

And neither did he.

Because it had always been there.

Even before she realized it.

22: A Love That Lived in the Smallest Moments

The world outside didn't exist here.
Not inside the penthouse.
Not inside the space that had become theirs without ever being spoken into existence.
Elena wasn't sure when she had stopped feeling like a guest.
She only knew that now, when she woke up in the mornings to the golden stretch of sunlight across the marble floors, when she heard the soft clink of a spoon against porcelain as Dominic stirred his coffee—she felt home.
Not in the walls.
Not in the breathtaking view of the city.
But in him.

A MORNING THAT MOVED Too Slowly

She stood by the window, wrapped in a light robe, watching as Dominic moved effortlessly through the kitchen.
He wasn't in a suit today.
Just a simple, fitted black sweater, sleeves rolled up to reveal strong forearms, a watch resting against the ridge of his wrist.
Elena's gaze lingered on the way he moved—with purpose, with quiet control.
Like everything he did, even something as simple as making breakfast, was done intentionally.
She didn't realize she was staring until Dominic turned.

And when he did—he looked directly at her.

A slow, knowing glance.

Her breath hitched.

"Come here." His voice was deep, smooth, effortlessly commanding.

Elena hesitated for half a second—but only half.

Then she moved.

A TOUCH THAT WASN'T Rushed

The moment she was close enough, Dominic reached for her.

Not in a way that was demanding.

Not in a way that asked for anything.

Just a slow, deliberate slide of his hand against her waist, pulling her just close enough to feel the warmth of his body.

Elena exhaled softly.

His fingers traced the knot of her robe, not untying it—just feeling it.

Then, with the faintest smirk, he murmured, "You didn't come for breakfast, did you?"

Heat bloomed in her cheeks.

She tried to pull away, but Dominic only hummed in amusement, his grip gentle but unyielding.

He let his other hand travel slowly up her spine, his fingertips pressing lightly against the back of her neck.

Elena shivered.

Her pulse fluttered as his thumb brushed against the curve of her jaw, tilting her chin up just slightly.

Not enough to claim her.

Just enough to make her want to be claimed.

THE FIRST KISS THAT Wasn't Enough

Elena barely had time to breathe before his lips touched hers.

Not demanding.

Not rushed.

Just a kiss that tasted like patience.

Like Dominic had waited long enough.

The world tilted slightly as he pulled her closer, deepening the kiss, his hand sliding through her hair, fingers curling at the base of her neck.

He tasted like black coffee and something undeniably him.

Something intoxicating.

Something she would never get enough of.

Her hands slid against his chest, feeling the warmth beneath the soft fabric of his sweater, the quiet strength in his body.

Dominic made a low sound against her lips, something close to approval.

Then—he broke the kiss.

But only to whisper against her mouth—

"Breakfast, Miss Rossi."

Her breath caught.

Because that wasn't a request.

That was a promise.

THE KIND OF MORNING Every Girl Dreams Of

The next hour passed in a slow blur.

Dominic moved around the kitchen with quiet ease, preparing breakfast while Elena perched on the counter, watching him.

It should have been ordinary.

It should have been simple.

But nothing about this love was ever ordinary.

She watched the way he handled the knife as he chopped, precise and controlled.

The way his brow furrowed slightly when he focused, as if even something as small as slicing fruit deserved his full attention.

The way he always—always—paused before handing her anything, just long enough to make sure her fingers brushed against his.

Every detail mattered.

Every moment lingered.

Because love wasn't in the grand declarations.

It was in the way he poured her coffee before making his own.

It was in the way he nudged a piece of fruit against her lips, watching her take a bite

like it was the most fascinating thing he had ever seen.

It was in the way his fingers grazed against her knee as he stood beside her—a touch so effortless yet so intimate, it sent a shiver up her spine.

By the time they finished eating, Elena wasn't sure if she was full or if she just didn't want to move.

Dominic leaned back in his chair, one hand resting against his jaw, watching her watch him.

Finally, after a long stretch of silence, he murmured, "What?"

Elena shook her head, her lips curving slightly. "Nothing."

Dominic smirked, but said nothing in return.

Because he knew.

They both knew.

There was nothing to say.

Because this was love.

A love that didn't need to be spoken.

A love that existed in the smallest, most perfect moments.

And neither of them were running from it anymore.

23: A Love That Needed No Proof

The world outside no longer mattered.
   Not in this space.
Not in the quiet rhythm of their mornings, the soft exchanges that needed no words.
Dominic never spoke of love.
But he showed it in every touch.
In every stolen glance.
In every moment he pulled her close without asking—because she had already chosen to stay.
And for the first time, Elena didn't question it.
Because some things didn't need proof.
Some things were simply felt.

THE TOUCH THAT MEANT Everything

Elena sat at the kitchen counter, stirring her coffee slowly.
Dominic stood across from her, sleeves rolled up, his watch resting against his wrist as he scrolled through his phone.
He looked as he always did—composed, unreadable.
But she knew better now.
Because his hand rested lightly against the counter, fingers just close enough to brush against hers every time she moved.
A touch so small, so effortless—but impossibly intimate.
Elena glanced at him, her heart tightening.
Does he even realize he does it?
Like it was instinct.

Like she had always belonged there.
Her fingers curled, testing something.
She pulled away—just an inch.
And in less than a second, Dominic shifted.
Closing the space between them again.
Not looking up.
Not acknowledging it.
Just undoing the distance.
Like being apart from her—**even by an inch—was unacceptable.
Her breath caught.
Because this wasn't something intentional.
This wasn't a calculated move.
This was love.
And he didn't even have to try.

THE MOMENT HE LET HIS Guard Down

Later that afternoon, the sky darkened with the promise of rain.

Elena sat curled against the couch, her legs tucked beneath her, flipping through a book.

She didn't hear Dominic approach.

But she felt him.

The warmth of him settling beside her, his presence quiet but unshakable.

She glanced up—and nearly stopped breathing.

Because for the first time, he wasn't guarded.

His tie was loose, the top buttons of his shirt undone, his hair slightly tousled like he had run his fingers through it too many times.

He looked like Dominic Moreau—but softer.

Like a version of himself he didn't show to the world.

Only to her.

Elena's heart ached.

Not with uncertainty.
With undeniable, breathtaking love.
She reached for him without thinking.
Her fingers brushed against his wrist—just a simple, delicate touch.
Dominic stilled.
Then—he moved.
Not in a rush. Not in demand.
Just a quiet, undeniable pull.
His hand lifted, fingers trailing along her jaw, tilting her face just enough for her to see the way his gaze darkened—not with control, but with something deeper.
Something unspoken.
And then—he kissed her.

THE KIND OF KISS THAT Stays Forever

It wasn't a demand.
It wasn't an ask.
It was a kiss that whispered of love without needing to say the words.
His lips moved against hers slowly, deeply—like he was memorizing her.
Like he wanted her to know that this was forever.
Elena's hands slid against his chest, feeling the slow, steady rhythm of his heartbeat beneath her fingertips.
Dominic exhaled softly, a sound of quiet surrender.
And in that moment—he wasn't untouchable.
He wasn't a man of power.
He was just a man in love.
Her man.
And she never wanted to be anywhere else.

A LOVE THAT WAS ALWAYS There

When the kiss finally ended, Dominic didn't move away.

He rested his forehead lightly against hers, his breathing slow, his fingers still tracing the curve of her jaw.

Elena's lips parted, as if she wanted to say something—but there was nothing left to say.

Because everything she needed to know was already there.

In his touch.

In his presence.

In every moment he had ever spent making sure she felt safe, wanted, loved.

He didn't need to tell her he loved her.

She already knew.

And when Dominic finally spoke, his voice low, unshaken, he didn't ask for permission.

He simply whispered—

"You're not going anywhere, Miss Rossi."

Elena didn't argue.

She just smiled.

And whispered back—

"I know."

Because this was love.

And she wasn't afraid of it anymore.

24: A Love That Didn't Need to Be Said

Elena had never believed in forever.
Not until now.
Not until Dominic Moreau had shown her that love wasn't about words—it was about presence.

He had never asked her to stay.

But in the way his fingers brushed against hers, in the way he always waited for her to move first, in the way his gaze softened when he looked at her—he had made it impossible for her to leave.

And Elena no longer wanted to.

MORNINGS THAT BELONGED to Them

She woke to the golden glow of morning, the faint hum of the city outside.

But what made her chest tighten—what made her heart ache in the best way—was the warmth beside her.

Dominic was already awake, lying on his side, his head propped up against his hand, watching her.

He didn't speak.

Didn't need to.

Because his gaze said everything.

Elena swallowed, her pulse unsteady. "How long have you been watching me?"

Dominic's lips twitched. "Long enough."

Her breath caught.

Because it wasn't teasing.

It was adoration.
The kind that wasn't fleeting, wasn't uncertain.
The kind that stayed.
She exhaled softly, shifting onto her side, mirroring him.
Dominic reached out, tucking a loose strand of hair behind her ear.
His fingers lingered—a slow, deliberate touch that made her entire body aware of his presence.
Elena swallowed.
He had touched her a hundred times before.
But **this—**this was something else.
Because this was love.
Unspoken, undeniable, and hers.

THE SOFTEST KIND OF Love
Neither of them moved for a long moment.
The world outside didn't exist.
Only them.
Only the soft press of Dominic's fingers as he traced them along her jaw, only the slow, steady rhythm of his breathing, only the warmth that existed in the small space between them.
Then, without a word, Dominic leaned in.
A kiss—not rushed, not demanding.
Just slow.
Just pure.
Just love.
Elena's fingers curled into the fabric of his shirt, grounding herself in him.
Dominic hummed softly, deepening the kiss just enough to make her sigh against his lips.
And when he pulled back—when his forehead rested against hers, his thumb brushing lightly against her cheek—she knew.

She had belonged to him long before she ever admitted it.
And now, there was no turning back.

BREAKFAST THAT WASN'T Just Breakfast

Dominic cooked.

Elena didn't know why it surprised her.

Of course he knew how to handle himself in a kitchen—Dominic Moreau didn't do anything without precision.

But there was something about watching him move so effortlessly, sleeves rolled up, the soft morning light making him look less like the man the world feared and more like the man she had fallen in love with.

Elena leaned against the counter, watching him.

Dominic glanced at her, one brow arching. "You're staring."

Elena smirked. "You like it."

Dominic hummed in amusement, placing a plate in front of her before stepping closer—so close that her breath caught.

His fingers trailed lightly along the inside of her wrist, sending a soft, delicious shiver down her spine.

Then, in a voice that was nothing more than a murmur, he whispered—"Eat, Miss Rossi."

Her stomach flipped.

Because it wasn't a command.

It was a promise.

A promise that she belonged here.

A promise that this wasn't fleeting.

A promise that he was hers.

And Elena never wanted to leave.

25: A Love That Felt Like Forever

Elena no longer questioned what this was.
She no longer hesitated when Dominic touched her, no longer wondered if she should pull away.
Because she didn't want to.
She had spent so long thinking love was something uncertain, something fragile.
But this—this wasn't fragile.
This was steady. Unshaken. Absolute.
And for the first time in her life, she let herself fall.

A DAY THAT FELT LIKE a Dream
They spent the day together without planning to.
No business meetings.
No interruptions.
Just them.
Dominic wasn't a man who wasted time, and yet—he moved slowly today.
Like he had nowhere else to be.
Like she was the only thing that mattered.
And Elena felt it.
In the way his fingers brushed against her lower back as they walked through the city.
In the way he paused before opening a door—just to glance at her, just to watch her.

In the way he touched her—not because he needed to, but because he couldn't help it.

It wasn't possessive.

It wasn't controlling.

It was love.

A love that didn't demand.

A love that didn't rush.

A love that had always been waiting for her to realize it was there.

A KISS THAT STOPPED Time

By the time they returned to the penthouse, the city lights had started to flicker to life, painting the walls in soft, golden hues.

Elena stepped inside first, sighing as she pulled off her coat.

Dominic followed, silent as always.

But when she turned—he was watching her.

Not with hunger.

Not with desire.

But with something deeper.

Something undeniable.

Elena's breath caught.

She barely had time to process it before he moved.

Slow. Deliberate.

His fingers brushed along the curve of her jaw, tilting her chin up—just enough to make her heart stutter.

She exhaled shakily. "Dominic—"

But he didn't let her finish.

Because his lips were on hers.

And suddenly, nothing else existed.

THE KIND OF LOVE THAT Stayed

This wasn't like the other kisses.

This one was unrushed.

It was soft, lingering.

Like Dominic had all the time in the world to memorize her.

Like he wasn't just kissing her.

Like he was claiming her in a way that needed no words.

Elena melted into him, her hands resting against his chest, feeling the slow, steady rhythm of his heart beneath her palms.

Dominic sighed against her lips—not in frustration, not in control, but in something dangerously close to surrender.

And that was enough.

More than enough.

Because this wasn't just love.

This was forever.

And she was ready to fall completely.

26: A Love That Wrapped Around Her

The morning light stretched softly across the room, golden and warm, but Elena was warmer.

Because Dominic Moreau's arm was draped across her waist, his presence wrapping around her even in sleep.

His breathing was deep, steady. Unshaken.

The world outside this bed—outside this moment—didn't exist.

And for the first time, Elena let herself surrender to it.

A MORNING THAT DIDN'T Rush

She shifted slightly, the silk sheets sliding against her skin.

And instantly—he moved.

Not awake. Not fully.

But his grip on her tightened—a quiet, instinctive reaction.

Like letting go wasn't an option.

Elena swallowed, her pulse stuttering.

Because this wasn't something intentional.

This was him.

Even in sleep, he needed her close.

And that did something to her chest—something she couldn't name.

Slowly, carefully, she turned.

And there he was.

Dominic.

Completely unreadable in the daylight.

Completely hers.

His hair was slightly tousled, the sharp angles of his face softened by the morning.

And for the first time, Elena wasn't afraid to touch him.

THE KIND OF TOUCH THAT Stayed

Her hand moved without thinking.

Fingers brushing against his jaw, tracing the line of his cheekbone, memorizing the way his skin felt beneath her touch.

She had never seen him like this.

Relaxed.

Unburdened.

Beautiful.

And then—his eyes opened.

Slowly. Like he had already known she was watching.

Elena's breath caught.

Because he wasn't unreadable anymore.

He was just looking at her.

The way a man looks at something he never wants to lose.

Her heart clenched.

"You're staring, Miss Rossi."

His voice was rough from sleep, quieter than usual, but just as devastating.

Elena exhaled a small laugh. "You like it."

Dominic smirked, but his fingers brushed against her wrist—trapping her hand against his skin.

Not letting her pull away.

Not letting her forget she was his.

Elena swallowed hard, her body warming beneath his gaze.

She should move.

She should breathe.

But then—Dominic lifted her hand to his lips.

And kissed her palm.
Soft. Unrushed.
The kind of kiss that sent something deep, aching, and dangerous through her chest.
A kiss that wasn't just a kiss.
It was a promise.
And Elena had no intention of breaking it.

A MORNING THAT SHOULDN'T Have Ended

They didn't move for a long time.
Dominic's fingers traced slow, lazy circles against her skin, as if memorizing her.
Elena let herself be held.
Let herself exist in his space.
Because this wasn't just passion.
This wasn't just longing.
This was love.
The kind that wrapped around her slowly, carefully, until she was drowning in it.
And she never wanted to come up for air.

27: A Love That Couldn't Be Undone

Elena wasn't sure when she stopped thinking about tomorrow.
   When she stopped questioning how long this would last.
All she knew was that this was now.
This was real.
And she didn't want it to end.

A DAY THAT FELT LIKE a Secret
   They spent the morning wrapped in silence.
   Not the heavy kind.
   Not the kind that begged to be filled.
   The kind that felt safe.
   Dominic wasn't the kind of man who wasted words.
   He didn't need to fill the air with unnecessary conversation, didn't need to say things just to hear himself speak.
   But he was always there.
   His hand resting against the small of her back as he passed her in the kitchen.
   His fingers brushing against hers as he handed her a cup of coffee.
   The way his gaze lingered—slow, deliberate, devastating.
   And Elena felt it.
   In every unspoken moment.
   In every touch that wasn't meant to claim her—only to remind her she was already his.

THE SOFTEST KIND OF Love

Later, as the afternoon stretched into golden light, they found themselves on the balcony.

The city hummed below them, alive and endless, but Elena didn't care.

Because her world wasn't out there.

It was here.

In him.

Dominic stood beside her, one hand resting casually against the balcony railing, his other wrapped around a glass of whiskey he had barely touched.

Elena didn't speak.

She just watched him, the sharp angles of his face softened in the sunlight, the quiet intensity of his presence unshaken.

And then—he turned.

His gaze found hers, something undeniable flickering behind his eyes.

A small, knowing smirk tugged at his lips.

"You're staring, Miss Rossi."

Elena exhaled a quiet laugh. "You like it."

Dominic didn't answer.

Not with words.

But his fingers lifted—**slow, intentional—**tucking a loose strand of hair behind her ear, his thumb lingering against her cheek just long enough to make her heart stutter.

Elena swallowed hard.

She should look away.

But she didn't.

Because he was looking at her like she was the only thing that had ever mattered.

And for the first time—she let herself believe it.

A LOVE THAT COULDN'T Be Ignored

Time blurred.

Minutes. Hours.

Elena didn't know how long they stood there.

All she knew was that Dominic never moved first.

He never pushed.

Never asked.

Because he knew she would come to him.

And she did.

Slowly. Deliberately.

Her fingers lifted, brushing lightly against the fabric of his sleeve, just to feel him.

Dominic exhaled softly, his eyes darkening—not with control, not with possession, but with something deeper.

Something unshakable.

And then—she kissed him.

Not in hesitation.

Not in question.

But in certainty.

Because this was love.

And she wasn't afraid of it anymore.

28: A Love That Stood Still

E lena had never believed in forever.
But now—she did.

Because forever wasn't a promise.

It wasn't something spoken, something written.

It was felt.

And in the quiet strength of Dominic's presence, in the way his touch never demanded, only offered—she felt it.

This wasn't just love.

This was certainty.

A MORNING THAT DIDN'T Rush

Elena stirred slowly, warmth wrapping around her before she even opened her eyes.

Not just the sheets.

Not just the soft glow of morning light filtering through the windows.

Him.

Dominic.

She turned slightly, and there he was.

Awake.

Watching her.

The golden light stretched across his face, making him look less untouchable, less unreadable.

More hers.

His hand rested against her waist, not pulling, not claiming—just there.

Like he had been waiting.

Like he always waited.

Elena exhaled softly. "You don't sleep much."

Dominic smirked. "You talk in your sleep."

Her stomach flipped.

Because this wasn't teasing.

It was something softer.

Something intimate.

Elena swallowed, watching him, her heart pounding too hard in her chest.

She should say something.

She should move.

But then—Dominic's fingers brushed against her jaw, tilting her chin up.

Not demanding.

Not rushing.

Just waiting.

And Elena moved first.

Her lips met his, slow and certain, because this time, she wasn't questioning it.

She wasn't questioning him.

THE KIND OF LOVE THAT Lingered

They stayed in bed too long.

Neither of them moved first.

Neither of them spoke.

Because some moments weren't meant to be interrupted.

Dominic's fingers traced slow, lazy patterns against her back, and Elena melted.

Not because he was powerful.
Not because he had built a world around her.
But because he had never asked her for anything.
And somehow—she wanted to give him everything.

A DAY THAT DIDN'T EXIST for Anyone Else

The hours passed in quiet certainty.
Dominic never asked if she was staying.
Because she already had.
The morning blurred into afternoon, and soon, Elena found herself standing in the kitchen, wrapped in one of his shirts, watching as he poured her coffee like he had done a hundred times before.
But this time felt different.
Because this wasn't new anymore.
This was theirs.
Dominic handed her the cup, and before she could take it—he paused.
And then—he kissed her.
Soft. Unrushed.
Like he had all the time in the world to memorize her.
Like she had always been his.
Elena exhaled, her fingers curling against his wrist, the warmth of his skin grounding her.
And when he pulled back—his gaze never wavered.
"Stay, Miss Rossi."
Not a request.
Not a command.
Just a truth he already knew.
And Elena—she already knew it, too.

29: A World That Demanded Perfection

Elena had seen glimpses of Dominic's power.
In the way people moved around him.
In the way doors opened before he reached them.
In the way silence carried his presence into every room.
But she had never questioned where it came from.
Until now.
Until the morning he handed her a gown.
And without a word—asked her to step into his world.

THE DRESS THAT WASN'T Just a Dress

It arrived in a box lined with silk, wrapped in precision.
Elena traced her fingers over the deep blue fabric, her breath catching at how impossibly smooth it felt beneath her touch.
Not just elegant.
Royal.
She glanced at Dominic, who stood a few feet away, sleeves rolled up, leaning casually against the counter.
Watching her.
Waiting.
"You expect me to wear this?" she asked.
Dominic tilted his head slightly, eyes glinting. "I expect you to be seen, Miss Rossi."
Her stomach tightened.
Because this wasn't just a dress.
This was a statement.

A declaration.

And she wasn't sure if she was ready for it.

A TRANSFORMATION SHE Never Saw Coming

The mirror didn't lie.

Elena barely recognized herself.

The gown clung to her frame, hugging her waist before falling into an effortless cascade of fabric—elegant, breathtaking.

The deep sapphire color made her skin glow, the soft shimmer catching the light like something untouchable.

The neckline dipped just enough to be daring, just enough to remind her she belonged in this world—even if she didn't believe it yet.

Dominic had chosen this for her.

Not by accident.

Not for vanity.

But because he wanted the world to look at her and see what he already knew.

That she was meant to be here.

She swallowed hard, smoothing her hands over the silk.

Then—she stepped out.

THE MOMENT HE SAW HER

She heard it before she saw him.

The soft clink of glass. The distant hum of the city through the open balcony doors.

And then—the silence.

She turned the corner, and there he was.

Standing in the middle of the room, a drink in one hand, the other tucked casually into his pocket.

His suit was perfectly tailored, the dark fabric sculpting against his frame effortlessly.

But his gaze—his gaze stole her breath.

Because Dominic Moreau didn't just look at her.

He devoured her.

Slow. Measured. Unshaken.

As if he was memorizing every detail.

As if the rest of the world had disappeared.

Elena's pulse hammered.

"Say something," she murmured.

Dominic took a slow sip of his drink, gaze never leaving hers.

Then, voice smooth and devastatingly quiet—

"You'll do."

Her breath caught.

Not at the words.

But at the way he said them.

Like there had never been a doubt.

Like she had always been meant to be here.

With him.

A CAR THAT FELT LIKE a Throne

The drive to the estate was quiet.

Not tense.

Not uncertain.

Just quiet.

Dominic sat beside her, his presence steady, unshakable.

Elena exhaled, staring out the window as the city faded into the background, replaced by vast, rolling land and a sky that stretched too far.

"Your family..." she started. "They know I'm coming?"

Dominic glanced at her, his expression unreadable.

"They know everything, Miss Rossi."
Her stomach twisted. "And do they approve?"
A pause.
Then, a faint smirk. "I never asked."
Elena swallowed.
Because this wasn't just a meeting.
This was a test.
And she wasn't sure if she would pass.

A HOUSE THAT WASN'T Just a House

The estate rose before them, a palace carved into time itself.
Not new.
Not modern.
Endless.
The kind of place built for legacy. For kings.
The car rolled to a slow stop, and before Elena could take a breath—the doors opened.
Not by the driver.
By the staff.
She barely had time to move before Dominic stepped out first, his presence shifting the air around him effortlessly.
Then, he turned.
And offered her his hand.
A simple gesture.
But a powerful one.
Because when she took it—there was no going back.

THE PEOPLE WHO HAD Always Watched Him

They were already waiting.

THE SILENT OATH

The grand entrance doors stood open, the soft glow of chandeliers spilling light onto the marble floors.

And in the center of it all—his family.

They didn't speak right away.

They didn't rush forward, didn't greet her with warmth.

They simply watched.

Assessed.

Judged.

And at the center—a woman.

Poised. Regal. Unshaken.

Her eyes met Dominic's first, something unspoken passing between them.

Then—her gaze flickered to Elena.

And held.

Elena's stomach tightened.

Because this wasn't just curiosity.

This was evaluation.

Then, finally, the woman spoke.

"So," she murmured, voice smooth and cool, *"you are the woman my son has chosen."

A pause.

Then—the smallest, knowing smile.

"Let's see if you were worth the trouble."

30: A Throne She Never Asked For

The moment Elena stepped inside, she felt it.
Power. Legacy. Expectation.
This wasn't just a family.
This was a dynasty.
And now—she was standing in the middle of it.

A SILENCE THAT WASN'T Empty

The grand hall was impossibly vast.
Golden chandeliers flickered overhead, casting soft shadows against centuries-old paintings that lined the walls.
Elena could feel their gazes—watching, waiting.
But she kept her back straight.
Kept her chin lifted.
Because she wasn't just here as Dominic's guest.
She was here as Dominic's choice.
And that meant something.
Even if she didn't know what yet.

THE WOMAN WHO HELD the Crown

The woman who had spoken first—Dominic's mother—moved forward.
She carried herself like someone who had never questioned her place in the world.

Like a queen who didn't need a title.
Elena swallowed.
She was beautiful. Impossibly elegant.

Dark hair pinned into a sleek chignon, diamonds resting against her collarbones, a gown tailored so perfectly it looked like it had been stitched onto her skin.

Everything about her presence was precise. Unshakable.
Her gaze never left Elena.
Then—she smiled.
Not warmly.
Not unkindly.
But in a way that told Elena she was already being measured.
"You wear the dress well," she said.
Elena's pulse quickened.
Because this wasn't a compliment.
It was a test.

A way of saying, I see what he did. Now let's see if you can wear more than just the fabric.

DOMINIC, UNMOVED

Elena barely had time to respond before Dominic spoke instead.
"She wears everything well."
His voice was smooth. Effortless. Unbothered.
Like he had already decided how this night would go.
Like no one else's opinion mattered.
And for the first time, Elena realized—
Dominic Moreau didn't bring her here to seek approval.
He brought her here to prove a point.
She was his.
And they could either accept it or be ignored.

THE UNSPOKEN WELCOME

Dominic's mother's lips curved slightly, as if amused by his response.

Then, with a small nod, she gestured toward the grand dining hall. "Shall we?"

Elena exhaled slowly.

And just like that—the night had begun.

A DINNER THAT WASN'T Just Dinner

The dining room was breathtaking.

A long, candlelit table stretched before them, flawlessly set with crystal glassware, polished silver, and gold-rimmed plates.

Servants moved like shadows, gliding in silence as they poured wine and placed courses before them.

Elena had never been anywhere like this.

Never sat among people who carried themselves not just with wealth, but with something bigger.

History. Power. Control.

She could feel it in the way they spoke, in the way they never truly looked at her—only at Dominic.

Because to them—he was the one who mattered.

And she was still an outsider.

A QUESTION THAT MEANT More Than It Seemed

Halfway through the meal, Dominic's mother set down her glass.

She hadn't spoken much.

But now—she looked at Elena fully.

"Tell me, Miss Rossi," she said, voice smooth. "What is it you do?"

Elena's stomach tightened.
Not because it was an unreasonable question.
But because it wasn't an innocent one.
This wasn't about small talk.
This was about placing her.
About seeing if she fit.
She could feel Dominic beside her, his presence calm, waiting.
Because he wasn't going to answer for her.
This was her moment.
She set her fork down carefully.
Lifted her chin.
And spoke.
"I build things."
A pause.
Then—the faintest flicker of interest.
"Build?"
Elena nodded, keeping her voice steady.
"I design interiors. Homes. Spaces. I take something empty and turn it into something that feels like it belongs."
The woman studied her for a moment.
Then—a smile.
Slow. Sharp.
"How fitting."
Elena's pulse hammered.
Because this wasn't a simple response.
This was a message.
One she wasn't sure she understood yet.

THE SHIFT IN POWER

The rest of the evening passed in quiet elegance.
Wine. Conversation.

Small, careful smiles that meant too much and not enough.
But by the time dessert was served, Elena realized something.
They weren't dismissing her.
Not completely.
They were watching.
Measuring.
Deciding.
Because this wasn't a rejection.
This was a test.
And Dominic already knew she would pass.

THE GOODBYE THAT WASN'T Final

As they stepped out into the crisp night air, Elena exhaled slowly, tension finally leaving her shoulders.

"That went better than expected," she murmured.

Dominic smirked. "Did it?"

Elena frowned. "Didn't it?"

Dominic didn't answer right away.

Instead, he lifted her hand to his lips—a slow, deliberate kiss against her fingers that sent a shiver through her.

Then, voice lower, quieter—

"They haven't decided yet, Miss Rossi."

A pause.

"But it doesn't matter."

She swallowed. "Why?"

Dominic's gaze darkened.

"Because I already have."

Her breath hitched.

And in that moment, Elena realized something.

She wasn't just standing beside Dominic Moreau.

She wasn't just in his world.

She was becoming a part of it.
And there was no turning back now.

31: A Test She Didn't Know She Was Taking

Elena had never been part of a world that required permission. She had built her life on independence, on making her own way.

But here—in Dominic's world—things were different.

And tonight, she realized something: it wasn't just about love.

It was about belonging.

And Dominic's family hadn't decided if she did.

THE MORNING AFTER

The sun had barely risen when Elena stirred.

She wasn't in the penthouse.

She was still here.

In a place that didn't yet feel like hers, surrounded by people who hadn't invited her.

Dominic was already awake.

She could feel it before she even opened her eyes.

The space beside her was warm but empty.

Elena sat up slowly, brushing her fingers through her hair as she glanced toward the open doors leading to the balcony.

And there he was.

Standing tall, dressed in a crisp white shirt, sleeves rolled up as he held a glass of dark whiskey in his hand.

Watching the world.

Or maybe—watching the war that had yet to come.

She exhaled softly. "You didn't sleep."

Dominic turned, his gaze settling on her.

"Not much."

His voice was smooth, but there was something else beneath it.

Something unspoken.

Something waiting.

Elena swung her legs over the edge of the bed, the silk sheets slipping from her shoulders.

"Was last night a test?" she asked.

Dominic's lips curved slightly, but he didn't answer.

Because they both knew the truth.

It wasn't just a test.

It was the beginning of something bigger.

And Dominic—he had known it all along.

THE BREAKFAST THAT Wasn't Just Breakfast

By the time Elena dressed and made her way downstairs, the estate was already awake.

Servants moved through the halls silently, efficiently

The scent of fresh coffee and warm pastries filled the air, but the tension beneath it was impossible to ignore.

She entered the grand dining hall, expecting a quiet morning.

Instead—they were all waiting.

Dominic sat at the head of the long table, perfectly at ease.

But beside him, across from him, along the stretch of polished wood—his family.

Watching her.

Measuring her.

Testing her.

Again.

Elena's pulse quickened.

But she didn't hesitate.
Didn't falter.
She walked forward, shoulders straight, chin lifted—just as Dominic had taught her.
And she took her seat.
Not because they had offered it.
But because it was hers now.

THE QUESTION THAT CHANGED Everything

The conversation was polite. Controlled.
Questions about her work. Her upbringing. Her past.
It was all carefully curated.
Until Dominic's mother placed her cup down, her gaze sharpening.
"Do you understand what it means to be here, Miss Rossi?"
Elena swallowed.
"To be with him?"
The air shifted.
She felt Dominic go still beside her.
But he didn't interrupt.
Didn't step in.
Because this was her moment.
Her chance to prove that she belonged.
She met the woman's gaze.
"It means I choose him."
A pause.
"And he chooses me."
The silence was deafening.
Then—Dominic smirked.
Soft. Subtle. Pleased.
Because she had passed.
At least for now.

THE GOODBYE THAT WASN'T a Goodbye

As they stepped outside, the crisp morning air wrapped around them.

The car waited.

Dominic's world was waiting.

And so was hers.

But as Elena turned, something unexpected happened.

Dominic's mother—the woman who had measured her, tested her, studied her—spoke.

"Elena."

Her name.

Not Miss Rossi.

Not the woman my son has chosen.

Just Elena.

She turned.

And for the first time—the woman smiled.

"We'll be seeing you again."

A pause.

"Soon."

Elena swallowed.

Because this wasn't a goodbye.

This was a beginning.

And whatever came next—she wasn't sure if she was ready.

But she would be.

Because she had already chosen this.

She had already chosen him.

And there was no turning back now.

32: A Throne That Came With a Price

The ride back to the city was silent.
    Not heavy.
Not uncertain.
Just full.
Full of the weight of what had happened.
Full of the shift that neither of them spoke about.
Full of the understanding that nothing would be the same.
Elena wasn't just a guest in Dominic's world anymore.
She was part of it.
And that—that changed everything.

THE RETURN TO A DIFFERENT Life

The car pulled up to the penthouse, and for the first time, it didn't feel like an escape.

It felt like the only place she belonged.

Dominic stepped out first, his presence still impossibly steady, unshaken.

Elena followed, exhaling softly as she walked inside, the familiar space wrapping around her like something safe.

Then, before she could even turn—

She felt him.

Dominic was behind her, close. Too close.

Not touching her.

Not yet.

But waiting.

Like he had waited for her to realize it on her own.
That this wasn't temporary.
That he had never doubted her.
That she was his.
Her breath hitched.
And when she turned to face him, his gaze—**steady, dark, devastating—**was already waiting for her.

THE MOMENT HE SAID Her Name

Dominic didn't speak.
Not at first.
But then—he did.
And for the first time, he didn't call her Miss Rossi.
He called her by her name.
"Elena."
It wasn't rushed.
It wasn't heavy.
It was soft.
Like something sacred.
Like something he had been waiting to say.
And Elena melted.
Because this—this was real.
Her fingers brushed against his jacket, feeling the heat of him beneath it.
He was warm.
Unshakable.
And hers.
Dominic lifted his hand, tracing his thumb along her jaw—not to claim, not to demand.
Just to remind her.

To remind her that he had always been waiting for her to see what he already knew.

That she belonged to him.

And finally—she did.

Elena inhaled sharply, her lips parting—

But before she could speak, he kissed her.

A KISS THAT SEALED Everything

Not rushed.

Not hesitant.

But slow.

Deep.

Final.

Like Dominic Moreau was telling the world that there was no one else.

Like he was telling her that there had never been anyone else.

Elena melted into him, her hands sliding against his chest, feeling the slow, steady rhythm of his heartbeat beneath her fingertips.

Dominic made a low sound against her lips—something quiet, something devastatingly real.

And when he pulled back—his forehead rested against hers.

Her breath was unsteady.

His wasn't.

Because he had always been sure.

Dominic exhaled softly.

"You should rest, Elena."

Elena swallowed.

"Why?"

His gaze darkened.

"Because things are about to change."

Her stomach twisted.

"And I need you ready."

33: A Storm Waiting to Break

Elena had always known that love wasn't just about passion.
It was about protection.
About belonging to something bigger than herself.
And now—she belonged to Dominic.
Which meant she was no longer untouchable.
Because if she was his...
Then she was theirs to destroy.

A MORNING THAT FELT Different

She woke to the scent of coffee.
The soft hum of the city beyond the glass walls.
And him.
Dominic stood near the window, one hand resting in his pocket, the other holding his cup, his gaze fixed on something she couldn't see.
Something outside.
Something waiting.
Elena sat up slowly, stretching beneath the sheets. "You're thinking too loud."
Dominic turned, his gaze steady, unreadable.
But then—his lips curved slightly.
"You slept through it."
Elena frowned. "Through what?"
Dominic took a sip of his coffee.
"The call."
Her stomach tightened. "What call?"

He didn't answer right away.

Instead, he placed his cup down, crossing the room in slow, measured steps.

By the time he reached the bed, Elena barely remembered how to breathe.

He lifted his hand, brushing his fingers through her hair, tilting her chin up just enough to make her heart stutter.

"Victor Laurent is gone."

Elena blinked. "What?"

"Disappeared," Dominic murmured, thumb tracing along her jaw. "No sightings. No calls. No trace of him anywhere."

A pause.

"But I don't believe in ghosts."

Elena swallowed. "You think he's planning something?"

Dominic exhaled softly. "I think he was never the real problem."

And for the first time, Elena felt it.

Not just the weight of his world.

But the war that was waiting beneath it.

THE ARRIVAL THAT CHANGED Everything

By noon, the penthouse was no longer quiet.

Men in suits moved in and out.

Security.

Elena didn't know their names.

Didn't need to.

Because they weren't here for her.

They were here for him.

For what was coming.

She stood near the balcony, watching as Dominic spoke in low, controlled tones with a man she had never seen before.

Broad. Dangerous-looking.

Someone who carried himself like he had seen things the rest of the world never would.

Elena stepped forward.

And instantly—Dominic's gaze snapped to her.

Not in warning.

Not in hesitation.

Just awareness.

Like he had felt her move before she even did.

Elena inhaled. "Tell me."

Dominic's jaw tensed.

The man beside him glanced at her, then back at Dominic. "She doesn't know yet?"

Dominic's gaze didn't waver. "Not everything."

Elena's pulse quickened. "Then tell me now."

Dominic studied her for a moment.

Then, slowly—he nodded.

"Go inside, Elena."

A pause.

"I'll explain everything."

And just like that—everything was about to change.

34: The Truth He Could No Longer Hide

Elena had always known Dominic was powerful.
But power wasn't just about money or influence.
Power was about control.
And for the first time—Dominic Moreau was about to lose his.
Because she wasn't waiting anymore.
She wanted the truth.
And this time—he was going to give it to her.

A ROOM WHERE NO LIES Could Exist

The penthouse was eerily quiet when Dominic closed the doors behind them.

Outside, his world was moving—his men, his security, the ones who lived in the shadows of his empire.

But here—it was just them.

Elena stood near the fireplace, arms crossed, her heart pounding.

"Tell me everything."

Dominic exhaled slowly, rolling back his sleeves, his movements controlled, measured.

Like a man preparing for a conversation he had never wanted to have.

"Where do you want me to start?"

Elena swallowed. "From the beginning."

Dominic's gaze darkened.

Then—he nodded.

And the truth finally came.

A NAME THAT WAS NEVER Meant to Be Spoken

"Victor Laurent was never the real problem."

Elena frowned. "Then who was?"

Dominic took a slow breath, stepping toward the window, his hands resting in his pockets.

"Victor was a distraction. A pawn."

"The real power?" His jaw tensed.

"That belongs to someone else."

Elena's stomach twisted. "Who?"

Dominic hesitated.

And then—he said the name.

A name that sent a chill through her skin.

A name that carried weight, history, danger.

A name that wasn't supposed to exist.

"Matthias Devereux."

Elena's pulse quickened. "Who is he?"

Dominic's gaze flickered to her, his expression unreadable.

"The man who wants to take everything from me."

A pause.

"And now, from you."

THE PRICE OF POWER

Elena barely breathed.

"Why?"

Dominic didn't answer immediately.

Instead, he stepped toward her.

Not rushed.

Not demanding.

But certain.

"Because he believes I took something from him first."
Elena swallowed. "And did you?"
Dominic held her gaze.
"No."
A pause.
"But I will."

THE WARNING THAT CAME Too Late

Before Elena could respond—Dominic's phone buzzed.

Sharp. Urgent.

He exhaled, pulling it from his pocket, answering without hesitation.

"What is it?"

A pause.

Then—a shift.

His body went still.

His grip on the phone tightened.

And when he finally spoke again—his voice was lethal.

"Where?"

Elena's breath caught.

"Dominic—"

He ended the call.

And when his eyes met hers, they were darker than she had ever seen them.

"Stay here."

Elena's stomach dropped. "What's happening?"

Dominic reached for his jacket. "Matthias just made his first move."

A pause.

"And I intend to end it before he makes another."

35: The First Move Was His

Dominic had spent his life calculating his every step.
Never reactive.
Never reckless.
Always in control.
But tonight—he wasn't waiting.
Because if Matthias Devereux wanted a war—then he had just started one.

A GOODBYE THAT WASN'T Really a Goodbye

Elena stood in front of the door, arms crossed, blocking his way.
"You're not going alone."
Dominic didn't flinch.
He didn't argue.
He simply tilted his head slightly, the way he always did when he was deciding whether to entertain a conversation or end it.
"Elena."
Just her name.
Soft. Final.
Her stomach twisted.
"You can't ask me to stay here and do nothing."
Dominic exhaled, his fingers brushing his watch—a small, almost unnoticeable movement.
But Elena had learned by now—nothing about him was unnoticeable.
"I'm not asking."

Her breath caught.
"I'm telling you."
And just like that—he stepped around her.
Effortless.
Certain.
Like nothing could stop him.
Like she was supposed to just let him go.
But she wasn't going to.
Not this time.

A PLAN HE DIDN'T SEE Coming

Elena wasn't reckless.
But she wasn't naive, either.
If Matthias Devereux was as dangerous as Dominic said—then he wouldn't just go after him.
He would come for both of them.
And Elena refused to be the weakness Dominic had to protect.
She reached for her phone, her pulse hammering.
There was someone who could help.
Someone who owed her.
And if Dominic wasn't going to let her in on his plan—then she would make her own.

THE MEETING THAT WASN'T Supposed to Happen

Dominic stepped into the warehouse—a place that had seen too many negotiations and too few survivors.
His men were already positioned.
Silent. Waiting.
And then—Matthias arrived.

Not with an army.
Not with an apology.
But with a smirk.
Like he had already won.
Like Dominic was already playing his game.
"Moreau."
Dominic didn't move.
Didn't blink.
He just watched. Waited.
Because the moment Matthias spoke—he had already lost.
"You came alone?" Matthias taunted. "Brave. Or foolish."
Dominic smirked.
"I don't make mistakes, Devereux."
A pause.
Then, in a voice lethal enough to steal the air from the room—
"But you just did."

36: The Moment the Game Changed

Dominic Moreau didn't make mistakes.
And yet—Matthias Devereux had just walked into one.
The warehouse was dark, the air thick with tension.
Matthias stood in the center, arms loose at his sides, his smirk laced with confidence.
Like he believed Dominic was already losing.
Like he had already won.
But the problem with men like Matthias?
They always thought they were playing chess.
When in reality—they were already checkmate.

A WARNING THAT WASN'T a Warning
"You should've stayed in the shadows, Devereux."
Dominic's voice was calm, unshaken.
Matthias exhaled a quiet laugh. "And miss the fun?"
His eyes flickered across the room, scanning for weaknesses.
Looking for an advantage.
And that was his first mistake.
Because there weren't any.
Dominic had built this moment.
Designed it.
And now—Matthias was exactly where he wanted him.

THE MOVE THAT SEALED It

A low buzz vibrated in Dominic's pocket.
One text. One confirmation.
It was done.
Matthias just didn't know it yet.
Dominic exhaled, rolling his sleeves up—slowly, deliberately.
Then, voice effortless, he murmured—
"You've already lost."
Matthias tensed. "What?"
Dominic smirked.
And just as the words left his lips—his phone buzzed again.
A second text.
From Elena.
Three words that changed everything.
"I found him."
Dominic's blood ran cold.
Because suddenly—Matthias wasn't the biggest problem in the room.
Elena was.

A MISTAKE HE DIDN'T See Coming

Dominic barely glanced at Matthias as he stepped back, pulling out his phone, his heartbeat pounding in his ears.
He called her.
One ring.
Two.
Then—her voice.
"Dominic."
Soft. Breathless.
And wrong.
Because there was something else in the background.
Something off.

"Elena." His voice sharpened. "Where are you?"

Silence.

Then—

"You're not the only one who can play games."

Not Elena's voice.

Matthias.

The line went dead.

And just like that—Dominic knew.

He had been so focused on the war he forgot to protect the only thing that mattered.

And now—Matthias had her.

37: A War That Just Became Personal

Dominic Moreau had spent his life controlling every outcome.

But now—the one thing he couldn't afford to lose was in someone else's hands.

And that was a mistake Matthias Devereux would not live to regret.

THE CALM BEFORE THE Storm

Dominic didn't rush.

He didn't panic.

Because men like him didn't react.

They destroyed.

His men stood around him, waiting for orders, tension crackling in the air like a storm ready to break.

But Dominic—he was already thinking ahead.

Matthias had Elena.

Which meant Matthias thought he had won.

But the real mistake wasn't taking her.

It was believing she was the weakness.

When in reality—she was the reason Dominic was about to end this.

ELENA WASN'T JUST WAITING

Elena's heart pounded as she sat in the dimly lit room, her wrists tied, her mind racing.

She wasn't afraid.

She was furious.

Matthias stood a few feet away, watching her with a smirk, his arrogance dripping from every movement.

"Moreau will come for you."

Elena exhaled, slow, steady.

"I know."

Matthias chuckled. "You sound so sure."

Elena tilted her head.

"Because I am."

A pause.

Then—she smiled.

And that was the moment Matthias should have realized—she wasn't scared.

Because Dominic wasn't just coming.

He was already here.

THE RECKONING BEGINS

The moment the first gunshot rang through the building, Matthias turned—but it was already too late.

Because Dominic Moreau didn't warn.

He didn't threaten.

He eliminated.

And tonight—he was here to burn this empire to the ground.

38: The Night Everything Changed

Dominic Moreau had spent his life eliminating threats before they became problems.

But this time—it was different.

Because Matthias Devereux had made one mistake too many.

He had taken Elena.

And now—Dominic was going to take everything from him.

A BATTLE THAT WAS ALWAYS Coming

The warehouse smelled of metal and dust, of old secrets buried beneath bloodstained floors.

Dominic stepped inside, his movements unhurried, precise—like a man who already knew the ending.

His men flanked him, shadows against the dim light.

But Dominic?

He was the real storm.

Matthias stood at the far end of the room, a gun resting lazily in his hand.

And beside him—Elena.

Her wrists were tied, but her expression was unshaken.

Because she knew.

Knew that Dominic was here.

Knew that this was over before it even began.

And when their eyes met—it was already decided.

She wasn't a victim.

She was his.

And he was about to take her back.

THE MOMENT IT ENDED
"You're late, Moreau."
Matthias smirked, tilting his head, as if he had control.
As if Dominic hadn't already stripped it from him.
Dominic's gaze never wavered.
"You're stalling."
A pause.
"Which means you've already lost."
Matthias's smirk faltered.
And in that fraction of hesitation—Dominic moved.
A gunshot.
A body hitting the floor.
A gasp—not Elena's.
And when the dust settled—Matthias Devereux lay still.
A man who had believed he was untouchable.
Until he met someone stronger.

A WAR THAT WASN'T OVER
Dominic untied Elena's wrists, his fingers brushing against her skin—a touch so gentle it stole her breath.
She exhaled shakily. "It's over."
Dominic's jaw tensed. "No."
She frowned. "Matthias is dead."
Dominic studied her, his gaze unreadable.
"He wasn't working alone."
Elena's stomach twisted.
"This war didn't end tonight."
A pause.

"It just started."

A NEW BEGINNING—AND a New Threat

They left the warehouse, but Dominic wasn't the same.

Something had shifted.

Because if Matthias wasn't the real power—then who was?

And more importantly—what was coming next?

Elena tightened her grip around Dominic's hand, her heart pounding.

She had stepped into this world believing she could walk away.

But now?

Now, there was no leaving.

Not for her.

Not for him.

And especially—not for the ones still hiding in the dark.

Because someone else was waiting.

Watching.

And as Dominic pulled her closer, his voice a whisper against her ear—she knew the war was far from over.

"I will burn the world before I let them take you again, Elena."

And this time—he meant it.

39: The End That Wasn't the End

The night was quiet.
Too quiet.
Elena stood by the window of the penthouse, staring out at the city below.
It should have been over.
Matthias Devereux was dead.
The war should have ended.
But deep down—she knew it hadn't.
Because power never disappears.
It just waits for the next one to take it.
And someone was waiting.
Watching.
Planning.
And when they made their move—Dominic would be ready.
Because this wasn't just about survival anymore.
This was about protecting what was his.
And Elena—she was his.

THE FINAL WORDS THAT Changed Everything
Dominic walked up behind her, his presence wrapping around her like something unshakable.
His fingers traced along her wrist, slow and deliberate.
"You're thinking too much."
Elena swallowed. "So are you."
Dominic smirked.

Then, voice softer, darker—
"It's not over."
She turned to face him. "I know."
A pause.
Then, in a voice so quiet it sent a shiver through her—
"Are you ready, Elena?"
Her pulse hammered.
Because this time, she wasn't afraid.
She lifted her chin.
"Always."
Dominic exhaled softly.
Then, brushing his lips against her temple—
"Then we begin."

Teaser for the Next Book

Coming Soon...

The Silent Oath was just the beginning.

A new threat looms. Secrets that should have remained buried begin to resurface.

And in the darkness, a shadow watches—waiting for the right moment to strike.

Elena thought she had escaped the past.

But the past isn't done with her.

Stay tuned for the next thrilling chapter in The Silent Oath series...